Anonymous

The Young Pilgrim

Anonymous

The Young Pilgrim

ISBN/EAN: 9783337294755

Printed in Europe, USA, Canada, Australia, Japan

Cover: Foto ©Andreas Hilbeck / pixelio.de

More available books at **www.hansebooks.com**

THE

YOUNG PILGRIM.

A Tale

ILLUSTRATIVE OF "THE PILGRIM'S PROGRESS."

BY

A. L. O. E.,

AUTHOR OF "THE SHEPHERD OF BETHLEHEM,"
"THE SILVER CASKET," ETC.

WITH ILLUSTRATIONS.

London:

T. NELSON AND SONS, PATERNOSTER ROW.

EDINBURGH; AND NEW YORK.

1887.

Preface.

I may perhaps be necessary to give a brief explanation of the object of this little work. It has been written as a CHILD'S COMPANION TO THE PILGRIM'S PROGRESS. That invaluable work is frequently put into youthful hands long before the mind can unravel the deep allegory which it contains; and thus its precious lessons are lost, and it is only perused as an amusing tale.

I would offer my humble work as a kind of *translation*, the term which was applied to it by a little boy to whom I was reading it in manuscript—a translation of ideas beyond youthful comprehension into the common language of daily life. I would tell the child, through the medium of a simple tale, that Bunyan's dream is a solemn reality, that the feet of the young may tread the pilgrim's path, and press on to the pilgrim's reward.

I earnestly wish that I had been able more completely
to carry out the object set before me; but difficulties
have arisen from the very nature of my work. I have
been obliged to make mine *a very free translation*, full
both of imperfections and omissions. This is more
especially the case where subjects are treated of in the
Pilgrim's Progress which concern the deeper experience
of the soul. Of fearful inward struggles and temptations, such as befell the author of that work, the gloom
and horrors of the Valley of the Shadow of Death, the
little ones who early set out on pilgrimage usually know
but little. They find the stepping-stones across the
Slough of Despond, and are rarely seized by Giant
Despair. It would be worse than useless to represent
the Christian pilgrimage as more gloomy and painful
than children are likely to find it.

There are other valuable parts of the Pilgrim's Progress, such as the sojourn in the House Beautiful, which
is believed by many to represent Christian communion,
which could hardly be enlarged upon in a design like
mine; while the present altered appearance of Vanity
Fair has compelled me to wander still further from my
original, if I would draw a picture that could be recog-

nized at the present day, and be useful to the rising generation.

Such as it is, I earnestly pray the Lord of pilgrims to vouchsafe his blessing on my little work. To point out to His dear children the holy guiding light which marks the strait gate and the narrow path of life, and bid them God speed on their way, is an office which I most earnestly desire, yet of which I feel myself unworthy. I may at least hope to lead my young readers to a nobler instructor, to induce them to peruse with greater interest and deeper profit the pages of the Pilgrim's Progress, and to apply to their own characters and their own lives the precious truths conveyed in that allegory.

A. L. O. E.

Contents.

List of Illustrations.

THE YOUNG PILGRIM.

CHAPTER I.

THE PILGRIM'S CALL.

" I dreamed, and, behold, I saw a man clothed with rags standing in a certain place, with his face from his own house, a book in his hand, and a great burden upon his back."—*Pilgrim's Progress.*

"IS this the way to the ruins of St. Frediswed's shrine?" said a clergyman to a boy of about twelve years of age, who stood leaning against the gate of a field.

"They are just here, sir," replied the peasant, proceeding to open the gate.

"Just wait a moment," cried a bright-haired boy who accompanied the clergyman ; "that is your way, this is mine," and he vaulted lightly over the gate.

"So these are the famous ruins !" he exclaimed as he alighted on the opposite side ; "I don't think much of them, Mr. Ewart. A few yards of stone wall, half

AT THE GATE.

covered with moss, and an abundance of nettles is all
I can see."

"And yet this once was a famous resort for pilgrims."

"Pilgrims,—what were they?" inquired the boy.

"In olden times, when the Romanist religion pre-
vailed in England, it was thought an act of piety to visit
certain places that were considered particularly holy;
and those who undertook journeys for this purpose
received the name of pilgrims. Many travelled thousands
of miles to kneel at the tomb of our Lord in Jerusalem,
and those who could not go so far believed that by visit-

ing certain famous shrines here, they could win the pardon of their sins. Hundreds of misguided people, in this strange, superstitious hope, visited the abbey by whose ruins we now stand; and I have heard that a knight, who had committed some great crime, walked hither barefoot, with a cross in his hand, a distance of several leagues."

"A knight barefoot! how strange!" cried young Lord Fontonore; "but then he believed that it would save him from his sins."

"Save him from his sins!" thought the peasant boy, who, with his full earnest eyes fixed upon Mr. Ewart, had been drinking in every word that he uttered; "save him from his sins! I should not have thought it strange had he crawled the whole way on his knees!"

"Are there any pilgrims now?" inquired Fontonore.

"In Romanist countries there are still many pilgrimages made by those who know not, as we do, the one only way by which sinners can be accounted righteous before a pure God. But in one sense, Charles, we all should be pilgrims, travellers in the narrow path that leads to salvation, passing on in our journey from earth to heaven, with the cross not in our hands but in our hearts; pilgrims, not to the tomb of a crucified Saviour, but to the throne of that Saviour in glory!"

Charles listened with reverence, as he always did when his tutor spoke of religion, but his attention was nothing compared to that of the peasant, who for the first time listened to conversation on a subject which had lately been filling all his thoughts.   He longed to speak, to ask questions of the clergyman, but a feeling of awe kept him back; he only hoped that the gentleman would continue to talk, and felt vexed when he was interrupted by three children who ran up to the stranger to ask for alms.

"Begging is a bad trade, my friends," said Mr. Ewart gravely, "I never like to encourage it in the young."

"We're so hungry," said the youngest of the party.

"Mother's dead, and father's broke his leg!" cried another.

"We want to get him a little food," whined the third.

"Do you live near?" asked Mr. Ewart.

"Yes sir, very near."

"I will go and see your father," said the clergyman.

The little rogues, who were accustomed to idle about the ruin to gain pence from visitors by a tale of pretended woe, looked at each other in some perplexity at the offer, for though they liked money well enough, they were by no means prepared for a visit.   At last Jack, the eldest, said with impudent assurance, "Father's not there, he's taken to the hospital, there's only mother at home."

"Mother! you said just now that your mother was dead."

"I meant—" stammered the boy, quite taken by surprise; but the clergyman would not suffer him to proceed
(193)

"Do not add another untruth, poor child, to those which you have just uttered. Do you not know that there is One above the heavens who hears the words of your lips, reads the thoughts of your hearts—One who will judge, and can punish?"

Ashamed and abashed, the three children made a hasty retreat. As soon as they were beyond sight and hearing of the strangers, Jack turned round and made a mocking face in their direction, and Madge exclaimed in an insolent tone, "We weren't going to stop for his sermon."

"There's Mark there that would take it in every word, and thank him for it at the end," said Jack.

"Oh, Mark's so odd!" cried Ben; "he's never like anybody else. No one would guess him for our brother!"

These words were more true than Ben's usually were, for the bright-haired young noble himself scarcely offered a greater contrast to the ragged, dirty children, than they with their round rustic faces, marked by little expression but stupidity on that of Ben, sullen obstinacy on Madge's, and forward impudence on Jack's, did to the expansive brow and deep thoughtful eye of the boy whom they had spoken of as Mark.

"Yes," said Jack, "he could never even pluck a wild-flower, but he must be pulling it to bits to look at all its parts. It was not enough to him that the stars shine to

give us light, he must prick out their places on an old
bit of paper, as if it mattered to him which way they
were stuck. But of all his fancies he's got the worst one
now ; I think he's going quite crazed."

"What's he taken into his head ?" said Madge.

"You remember the bag which the lady dropped at
the stile, when she was going to the church by the
wood ?"

Madge nodded assent, and her brother continued :
"What fun we had in carrying off and opening that bag,
and dividing the things that were in it ! Father had the
best of the fun of it though, for he took the purse with
the money."

"I know," cried Ben, "and mother had the handkerchief with lace round the edge, and E. S. marked in the
corner. We—more's the shame !—had nothing but some
pence, and the keys ; and Mark, as the biggest, had the
book."

"Ah ! the book !" cried Jack ; "that's what has put
him out of his wits !"

"No one grudged it him, I'm sure," said Ben, "precious little any of us would have made out of it. But Mark
takes so to reading, it's so odd ; and it sets him a thinking, a thinking : well, I can't tell what folk like us have
to do with reading and thinking !"

"Nor I !" cried both Madge and Jack.

"I shouldn't wonder," said the latter, as stretched on

the grass he amused himself with shying stones at the sparrows, "I shouldn't wonder if his odd ways had something to do with that red mark on his shoulder!"

"What, that strange mark, like a cross, which made us call him the Red-cross Knight, after the ballad which mother used to sing us?"

"Yes; I never saw a mark like that afore, either from blow or burn."

"Mother don't like to hear it talked of," said Madge.

"Well, whatever has put all this nonsense into his head, father will soon knock it out of him when he comes back!" cried Jack. "He's left off begging,—he won't ask for a penny, and he used to get more than we three together, 'cause ladies said he looked so interesting ; and he'll not so much as take an egg from a nest,—he's turned quite good for nothing!"

Leaving the three children to pursue their conversation, we will return to him who was the subject of it. That which had made them scoff had made him reflect,—he could not get rid of those solemn words, "There is One above the heavens who hears the words of your lips, reads the thoughts of your hearts—One who will judge, and can punish!" They reminded him of what he had read in his book, *The soul that sinneth it shall die;* he knew himself to be a sinner, and he trembled.

Little dreaming what was passing in the mind of the peasant, Mr. Ewart examined the ruin without noticing him further, and Mark still leant on the gate, a silent, attentive listener.

"I think, Charles," said the tutor, "that I should like to make a sketch of this spot, I have brought my paint-box and drawing block with me, and if I could only pro-cure a little water—"

"Please may I bring you some, sir?" said Mark.

The offer was accepted, and the boy went off at once, still turning in his mind the conversation that had passed.

"'Pilgrims in the narrow path that leadeth to salva-tion,'—I wish that I knew what he meant. Is that a path only for holy men like him, or can it be that it is open to me? Salvation! that is safety, safety from punishment, safety from the anger of the terrible God. Oh, what can I do to be saved!"

In a few minutes Mark returned with some fresh water which he brought in an old broken jar. He set it down by the spot where Mr. Ewart was seated.

"Thanks, my good lad," said the clergyman, placing a silver piece in his hand.

"Good," repeated Mark to himself; "he little knows to whom he is speaking."

"It would be tedious to you, Charles, to remain beside me while I am sketching," said Mr. Ewart; "you will enjoy a little rambling about; only return to me in an hour."

"I will explore!" replied the young lord gaily;

"there is no saying what curiosities I may find to remind me of the pilgrims of former days."

And now the clergyman sat alone, engaged with his paper and brush, while Mark watched him from a little distance, and communed with his own heart.

"He said that he knew the one, only way by which sinners could be accounted righteous—righteous! that must mean good—before a holy God! He knows the way; oh, that he would tell it to me! I have half a mind to go up to him now; it would be a good time when he is all by himself." Mark made one step forward, then paused. "I dare not, he would think it so strange. He could not understand what I feel. He has never stolen, nor told lies, nor sworn; he would despise a poor sinner like me. And yet," added the youth with a sigh, "he would hardly sit there, looking so quiet and happy, if he knew how anxious a poor boy is to hear of the way of salvation, which he says that he knows. I will go nearer; perhaps he may speak first."

Mr. Ewart had begun a bold, clever sketch,—stones and moss, trees and grass were rapidly appearing on the paper, but he wanted some living object to give interest to the picture. Naturally his eye fell upon Mark, in his tattered jacket and straw hat, but he forgot his sketch as he looked closer at the boy, and met his sad, anxious gaze.

"You are unhappy, I fear," he said, laying down his pencil.

Mark cast down his eyes, and said nothing.

" You are in need, or you are ill, or you are in want of a friend," said the clergyman with kind sympathy in his manner.

" Oh, sir, it is not that—" began Mark, and stopped.

" Come nearer to me, and tell me frankly, my boy, what is weighing on your heart. It is the duty, it is the privilege of the minister of Christ to speak comfort to those who require comfort."

" Can you tell me," cried Mark, with a great effort, " the way for sinners—to be saved ? "

" The Saviour is *the Way, the Truth, and the Life*, the Gate by which alone we enter into salvation. *Believe on the Lord Jesus Christ and thou shalt be saved. The just shall live by faith.*"

" What is faith ? " said Mark, gathering courage from the gentleness with which he was addressed.

" Faith is to believe all that the Bible tells us of the Lord, His glory, His goodness, His death for our sins, to believe all the promises made in His Word, to rest in them, hope in them, make them our stay, and love Him who first loved us. Have you a Bible, my friend ? "

" I have."

" And do you read it ? "

" Very often," replied Mark.

" *Search the Scriptures*, for they are the surest guide; search them with faith and prayer, and the Lord will not leave you in darkness, but guide you by his counsel here, and afterward receive you to glory."

Mr. Ewart did not touch his pencil again that day, his sketch lay forgotten upon the grass. He was giving his hour to a nobler employment, the employment worthy of angels, the employment which the Son of God Himself undertook upon earth. He was seeking the sheep lost in the wilderness, he was guiding a sinner to the truth.

" I hope that I have not kept you waiting," exclaimed Charles, as he came bounding back to his tutor ; " the carriage has come for us from the inn ; it looks as if we should have rain, we must make haste home."

Mr. Ewart, who felt strongly interested in Mark, now asked him for his name and address, and noted down both in his pocket-book. He promised that, if possible, he would come soon and see him again.

" Keep to your good resolutions," said the clergyman, as he walked towards the carriage, accompanied by Charles ; " and remember that though *the just shall live by faith*, it is such faith as must necessarily produce *repentance, love,* and *a holy life.*"

Mr. Ewart stepped into the carriage, the young lord sprang in after him, the servant closed the door and they drove off. Mark stood watching the splendid equipage as it rolled along the road, till it was at last lost to his sight.

"I am glad that I have seen him—I am so glad that he spoke to me—I will never forget what he said! Yes, I will keep to my good resolutions; from this hour I will be a pilgrim to heaven, I will enter at once by the strait gate, and walk in the narrow way that leadeth unto life!"

CHAPTER II.

DIFFICULTIES ON SETTING OUT.

" They drew nigh to a very miry slough, that was in the midst of the plain ; and they being heedless, did both fall suddenly into the bog. The name of the slough was Despond."—*Pilgrim's Progress.*

EVENING had closed in with rain and storm, and all the children had returned to the cottage of their mother. A dirty, uncomfortable abode it looked, most unlike those beautiful little homes of the peasant which we see so often in dear old England, with the ivy-covered porch, and the clean-washed floor, the kettle singing merrily above the cheerful fire, the neat rows of plates ranged on the shelf, the prints upon the wall, and the large Bible in the corner.

No; this was a cheerless-looking place, quite as much from idleness and neglect as from poverty. The holes in the window were stuffed with rags, the little garden in front held nothing but weeds, the brick floor appeared as though it had never been clean, and everything lay about in confusion. An untidy-looking woman, with

her shoes down at heel, and her hair hanging loose
about her ears, had placed the evening meal on the
table; and round it now sat the four children, busy
with their supper, but not so busy as to prevent a
constant buzz of talking from going on all the time
that they ate.

"I say, Mark," cried Jack, "what did the parson
pay you for listening to him for an hour?"

"How much did you get out of him?" said Madge.

"Any money?" asked Ann Dowley, looking up
eagerly.

Mark laid sixpence on the table.

"I daresay that you might have got more," said
Ben.

"I did get more—but not money."

"What, food, or clothes, or—"

"Not food, nor clothes, but good words, which were
better to me than gold."

This announcement was received with a roar of
laughter, which did not, however, disconcert Mark.

"Look you," he said, as soon as they were sufficiently
quiet to hear him, "look you if what I said be not
true. You only care for things that belong to this life,
but it is no more to be compared to the life that is to
come than a candle to the sun, or a leaf to the forest!
Why, where shall we all be a hundred years hence?"

"In our graves, to be sure," said Ben.

"That is only our bodies—our poor, weak bodies; but our souls, that think, and hope, and fear, where will they be then?"

"We don't want to look on so far," observed Jack.

"But it may not be far," exclaimed Mark. "Thousands of children die younger than we, there are many, many small graves in the churchyard ; death may be near to us, it may be close at hand, and *where will our souls be then ?*"

"I don't know," said Madge; "I don't want to think," subjoined her elder brother ; their mother only heaved a deep sigh.

"Is it not something," continued Mark, "to hear of the way to a place where our souls may be happy when our bodies are dust ? Is it not something to look forward to a glorious heaven, where millions and millions of years may be spent amongst joys far greater than we can think, and yet never bring us nearer to the end of our happiness and glory ?"

"Oh, these are all dreams," laughed Jack, "that come from reading in that book."

"They are not dreams!" exclaimed Mark, with earnestness, "they are more real than anything on earth. Everything is changing here, nothing is sure ; flowers bloom one day and are withered the next ; now there is sunshine, and now there is gloom ; you see a man strong and healthy, and the next thing you hear of him perhaps is his death! All things are changing and passing away, just like a dream when we awake; but heaven and its delights are sure, quite sure; the rocks may be moved—but it never can be changed; the sun may be darkened—it is all bright for ever!"

"Oh that we might reach it!" exclaimed Ann Dowley, the tears rising into her eyes. Her sons looked at her in wonder, for they had never known their mother utter such a sentence before. To them Mark's enthusiasm seemed folly and madness, and they could not hide their surprise at the effect which it produced upon one so much older than themselves.

Ann Dowley had been brought up to better things, and had received an education very superior to the station in which she had been placed by her marriage. For many years she had been a servant in respectable families, and though all was now changed—how miserably changed!—she could not forget much that she had once seen and heard. She was not ignorant, though low and coarse-minded, and it was perhaps from this circumstance that her family were decidedly more intelligent than country children of their age usually are. Ann could read well, but her only stock of books consisted of some dirty novels, broken-backed and torn—she would have done well to have used them to light the fire. She was one who had never cared much for religion, who had not sought the Creator in the days of

her youth ; but she was unhappy now, united to a husband whom she dreaded, and could not respect—whose
absence for a season was an actual relief; she was poor,
and she doubly felt the sting of poverty from having
once been accustomed to comfort—and Mark's description of peace, happiness, and joy, touched a chord in her
heart that had been silent for long.

MARK AND HIS MOTHER.

"You too desire to reach heaven!" cried Mark, with
animation sparkling in his eyes; "oh, mother, we will
be pilgrims together, struggle on together in the narrow
way, and be happy for ever and ever!"

The three younger children, who had no taste for conversation such as this, having finished their meal slunk into the back room, to gamble away farthings as they had learned to do from their father. Ann sat down by the fire opposite to Mark, a more gentle expression than usual upon her face, and pushing back the hair from her brow, listened, leaning on her hand.

"I will tell you, mother, what the clergyman told me—I wish that I could remember every word. He said that God would guide us by his counsel here, and afterward receive us to glory. And he spoke of that glory, that dazzling, endless glory! Oh, mother, how wretched and dark seems this earth when we think of the blessedness to come!"

"But that blessedness may not be for us," said Ann.

"He said that it was for those who had faith, who believed in the Lord Jesus Christ."

"I believe," said the woman, "I never doubted the Bible; I used to read it when I was a child."

"We will read mine together now, mother."

"And what more did the clergyman tell you?"

"He told me that the faith which brings us to heaven will be sure to produce—" Mark paused to recall the exact words—"repentance, love, and a holy life."

"A holy life!" repeated Ann, slowly. Painful thoughts crossed her mind of many things constantly done that ought not to be done, habits hard to be parted with as a right hand or a right eye; holiness seemed something as far beyond her reach as the moon which was now rising in the cloudy sky; she folded her hands with a gloomy smile, and said, "If *that* be needful, we may as well leave all these fine hopes to those who have some chance of winning what they wish!"

"The way is not shut to us."

"I tell you that it is," said the woman, impatiently; for the little gleam of hope that had dawned on her soul had given place to sullen despair. "To be holy you must be truthful and honest—we are placed in a situation where we cannot be truthful, we cannot be honest, we cannot serve God! It is all very well for the rich and the happy; the narrow way to them may be all strewed with flowers, but to us it is closed—and for ever!" She clenched her hand with a gesture of despair.

"But, mother—"

"Talk no more," she said, rising from her seat; "do you think that your father would stand having a saint for his wife, or his son! We have gone so far that we cannot turn back, we cannot begin life again like children—never speak to me again on these matters!" and, so saying, Ann quitted the room, further than ever from the strait gate that leadeth unto life, more determined to pursue her own unhappy career.

The heart of Mark sank within him. Here was disappointment to the young pilgrim at the very outset: fear, doubt, and difficulty enclosed him round, and hope was but as a dim, distant light before him. But help seemed given to the lonely boy, more lonely amid his unholy companions than if he had indeed stood by himself in the world. He looked out on the pure, pale moon in the heavens: the dark clouds were driving across her path, sometimes seeming to blot her from the sky; then a faint, hazy light would appear from behind them; then a slender, brilliant rim would be seen; and at last the full orb would shine out in glory, making even the clouds look bright!

"See how these clouds chase each other, and crowd round the moon, as if they would block up her way!" thought Mark. They are like the trials before me now, but bravely she keeps on her path through all and I must not—I will not despair!"

CHAPTER III.

" Now as Christian was walking solitarily by himself, he espied one afar off come crossing over the field to meet him; and their hap was to meet just as they were crossing the way of each other. The gentleman's name that met him was Mr. Worldly Wiseman."—*Pilgrim's Progress*.

THE bright morning dawned upon Holyby, the storm had spent itself during the night, and nothing remained to mark that it had been but the greater freshness of the air, clearness of the sky, and the heavy moisture on the grass that sparkled in the sun.

As the young pilgrim sat under an elm-tree, eating the crust which served him for a breakfast, and meditating on the events and the resolutions of the last day, Farmer Joyce came riding along the road, mounted on a heavy horse which often did service in the plough, and drew up as he reached the boy.

" I say, Mark Dowley," he called in a loud, hearty voice, "you are just the lad I was looking for!"

" Did you want me?" said Mark, raising his eyes.

"Do you know Mr. Ewart?" cried the farmer; and on Mark's shaking his head, continued, "why, he was talking to me about you yesterday—a clergyman, a tall man with a stoop—he who is tutor to Lord Fontonore."

"Oh, yes!" cried Mark, springing up, "but I did not know his name. What could he be saying of me?"

"He stopped at my farm on his drive home yesterday, and asked me if I knew a lad called Mark Dowley, and what sort of character he bore. Says I," continued the farmer, with a broad smile on his jovial face, "I know nothing against that boy in particular, but he comes of a precious bad lot!"

"And what did he reply?" cried Mark, eagerly.

"Oh, a great deal that I can't undertake to repeat, about taking you out of temptation, and putting you in an honest way; so the upshot of it is that I agreed to give you a chance, and employ you myself to take care of my sheep, to see if anything respectable can be made of you."

"How good in him—how kind!" exclaimed Mark.

"It seems that you got round him—that you found his weak side, young rogue! You had been talking to him of piety and repentance, and wanting to get to heaven. But I'll give you a word of advice, my man, better than twenty sermons. You see I'm thriving and prosperous enough, and well respected, though I should not say so, and I never wronged a man in my life. If you would be the same, just mind what I say, keep the commandments, do your duty, work hard, owe nothing, and steer clear of the gin-shop, and depend upon it you'll be happy now, and be sure of heaven at the last."

"Mr. Ewart said that by faith—"

"Faith!" exclaimed the farmer, not very reverently; "don't trouble yourself with things quite above you—things which you cannot understand. It is all very well for a parson like him—a very worthy man in his way, I believe, but with many odd, fanciful notions. My religion is a very simple one, suited to a plain man like me; I do what is right, and I expect to be rewarded; I go on in a straightforward, honest, industrious way, and I feel safer than any talking and canting can make one. Now you mind what you have heard, Mark Dowley, and come up to my farm in an hour or two. I hope I'll have a good account to give of you to the parson; and the young lord, he too seemed to take quite an interest in you."

"Did he?" said Mark, somewhat surprised.

"Yes, it's odd enough, with such riches as he has, one would have thought that he had something else to think of than a beggar boy. Why, he has as many thousands a-year as there are sheaves in that field!"

"He had a splendid carriage and horses."

"Carriage! he might have ten for the matter of that. They say he has the finest estate in the county of York;

but I can't stay here idling all day," added the farmer;
"you come up to my place as I said, and remember all
you've heard to-day. I have promised to give you a
trial; but mark me, my lad, if I catch you at any of
your old practices, that moment you leave my service.
So, *honesty is the best policy*, as the good old proverb
says." With that he struck his horse with the cudgel
which he carried in his hand, and went off at a slow,
heavy trot.

"There is a great deal of sense in what he has said,"
thought Mark, as he turned in the direction of Anne's
cottage to tell her of his new engagement. " 'Keep the
commandments, work hard, and steer clear of the gin-
shop, and you'll be sure of heaven at the last!' These
are very plain directions any way, and I'm resolved to
follow them from this hour. Some of my difficulties
seem clearing away; by watching the sheep all the day
long I shall be kept from a good many of my temptations. I shall have less of the company of my brothers,
I shall earn my bread in an honest way, and yet have
plenty of time for thought. 'Keep the commandments,'
let me think what they are;" and he went over the ten
in his mind, as he learned them from his Bible. "I
think that I may manage to keep them pretty strictly,
but there are words in the Word of God which will
come to my thoughts. *A new commandment I give
you, that ye love one another:* and, *He that hateth his*

brother is a murderer;—how can I love those who dislike me ?—'tis impossible ; I don't believe that any one
could."

The first thing that met the eyes of Mark on his
entering the cottage put all his good resolutions to flight.
Jack and Ben were seated on the brick floor, busy in
patching up a small broken box, and as they wanted
something to cut up for a lid, they had torn off the
cover from his beautiful Bible, and thrown the book itself under the table ! Mark darted forward with an
oath—alas ! his lips had been too long accustomed to
such language for the habit of using it to be easily
broken, though he never swore except when taken by
surprise, as in this instance. He snatched up first the
cover, and then the book, and with fiery indignation
flashing in his eyes, exclaimed, "I'll teach you how to
treat my Bible so !"

" *Your* Bible !" exclaimed Ben, with a mocking laugh ;
" Mark thinks it no harm to steal a good book, but it's
desperate wicked to pull off its cover !"

" Oh, that's what the parson was teaching him !" cried
Jack. Provoked beyond endurance, Mark struck him.

"So it's that you're after !" exclaimed Jack, springing up like a wild cat, and repaying the blow with interest. He was but little younger than Mark, and of
much stronger make, therefore at least his match in a
struggle. The boys were at once engaged in fierce

fight, while Ben sat looking on at the unholy strife, laughing, and shouting, and clapping his hands, and hallooing to Jack to "give it him!"

"What are you about there, you bad boys?" exclaimed Ann, running from the inner room at the noise of the scuffle. Jack had always been her favourite son, and without waiting to know who had the right in the dispute, she grasped Mark by the hair, threw him violently back, and, giving him a blow with her clenched hand, cried, "Get away with you, sneaking coward that you are, to fight a boy younger than yourself!"

"You always take his part, but he'll live to be your torment yet!" exclaimed Mark, forgetting all else in the blind fury of his passion.

"He'll do better than you, with all your canting," cried Ann. The words in a moment recalled Mark to himself; what had he been doing? what had he been saying? he, the pilgrim to heaven; he, the servant of God! With a bitterness of spirit more painful than any wrong which could have been inflicted upon him by another, he took up the Bible which had been dropped in the struggle, and left the cottage without uttering a word.

Mortifying were Mark's reflections through that day, as he sat tending his sheep. "Keep the commandments!" he sadly murmured to himself; "how many have I broken in five minutes! I took God's name in vain—a terrible sin. It is written, *Above all things*

HERDING SHEEP.

swear not. I did not honour my mother, I spoke iu-solently to her. I broke the sixth commandment by hating my brother; I struck him; I felt as though I could have knocked him down and trampled upon him! How can I reach heaven by keeping the commandments? I could as well get up to those clouds by climbing a tree. Well, but I'll try once again, and not give up yet. There is no one to provoke me, no one to tempt me here; I can be righteous at least when I am by myself."

So Mark sat long, and read in his Bible, mended it as well as he could, and thought of Mr. Ewart and his words. Presently his mind turned to Lord Fontonore, the fair, bright-haired boy who possessed so much wealth, who was placed in a position so different from his own.

"He must be a happy boy indeed!" thought Mark, "with food in abundance, every want supplied, not knowing what it is to wish for a pleasure and not have it at once supplied. He must be out of the way of temptation too, always under the eye of that kind, holy man, who never would give a rough word, I am sure, but would always be leading him right. It is very hard that there are such differences in the world, that good things are so very unevenly divided. I wish that I had but one quarter of his wealth; he could spare it, no doubt, and never feel the loss." Without thinking what he was doing, Mark turned over a leaf of the Bible which lay open upon his knee. *Thou shalt not covet*, were the first words that met his gaze; Mark sighed heavily, and closed the book.

"So, even when I am alone, I am sinning still; coveting, repining, murmuring against God's will, with no more power to stand upright for one hour than this weed which I have plucked up by the roots. And yet *the soul that sinneth it shall die*. I cannot get rid of these terrible words. I will not think on this subject any more, it only makes me more wretched than I was. Oh! I never knew, till I tried it to-day, how hard, how impossible it is to be righteous before a holy God!"

So, tempted to banish the thought of religion altogether from his mind, because he felt the law to be too holy to be kept unbroken, yet dreading the punishment for breaking it, Mark tried to turn his attention to other things. He watched the sheep as they grazed, plucked wild-flowers and examined them, and amused himself as best he might.

The day was very hot, there was little shade in the field, and Mark grew heated and thirsty. He wished that there were a stream running through the meadow, his mouth felt so parched and dry.

On one side of the field there was a brick wall, dividing it from the garden belonging to Farmer Joyce. On the top of this grew a bunch of wild wall-flower, and Mark, who was particularly fond of flowers, amused himself by devising means to reach it. There was a small tree growing not very far from the spot, by climbing which, and swinging himself over on the wall, he thought that he might succeed in obtaining the prize. It would be difficult, but Mark rather liked difficulties of this sort, and anything at that time seemed pleasanter than thinking.

After one or two unsuccessful attempts, the boy found

himself perched upon the wall; but the flower within his reach was forgotten. He looked down from his height on the garden below, with its long lines of fruit-bushes, now stripped and bare, beds of onions, rows of beans, broad tracts of potatoes, all the picture of neatness and order. But what most attracted the eye of the boy was a splendid peach-tree, growing on the wall just below him, its boughs loaded with rich tempting fruit. One large peach, the deep red of whose downy covering showed it to be so ripe that one might wonder that it did not fall from the branch by its own weight, lay just within reach of his hand. The sight of that fruit, that delicious fruit, made Mark feel more thirsty than ever. He should have turned away, he should have sprung from the wall; but he lingered and looked, and looking desired, then stretched out his hand to grasp. Alas for his resolutions! alas for his pilgrim zeal! Could so small a temptation have power to overcome them?

Yet let the disadvantages of Mark's education be remembered: he had been brought up with those to whom robbing an orchard seemed rather a diversion than a sin. His first ardour for virtue had been chilled by failure; and who that has tried what he vainly attempted does not know the effect of that chill? With a hesitating hand Mark plucked the ripe peach; he did not recollect that it was a similar sin which once plunged the whole earth into misery—that it was tasting forbidden fruit which brought sin and death into the world. He raised it to his lips, when a sudden shout from the field almost caused him to drop from the wall.

"Holloa there, you young thief! Are you at it already? Robbing me the very first day! Come down, or I'll bring you to the ground with a vengeance!" It was the angry voice of the farmer.

Mark dropped from his height much faster than he had mounted, and stood before his employer with his face flushed to crimson, and too much ashamed to lift up his eyes.

"Get you gone," continued the farmer, "for a hypocrite and a rogue; you need try none of your canting on me. Not one hour longer shall you remain in my employ; you're on the high road to the gallows."

Mark turned away in silence, with an almost bursting heart, and feelings that bordered on despair. With what an account of himself was he to return to his home, to meet the scoffs and jests which he had too well deserved? What discredit would his conduct bring on his religion! How his profane companions would triumph in his fall! The kind and pitying clergyman would regard him as a hypocrite—would feel disappointed in him. Bitter was the thought. All his firm resolves had snapped like thread in the flame, and his hopes of winning heaven had vanished.

CHAPTER IV.

" Ye cannot be justified by the works of the law; for by the deeds of the law no man living can be rid of his burden."--Pilgrim's Progress.

"WHAT ails you my young friend?—has anything painful happened?" said a kindly voice, and a hand was gently laid upon the shoulder of Mark, who was lying on the grass amidst the ruins of the old Abbey, his face leaning on his arms, and turned towards the earth, while short convulsive sobs shook his frame.

"Oh, sir!" exclaimed Mark, as a momentary glance enabled him to recognize Mr. Ewart.

"Let me know the cause of your sorrow," said the clergyman, seating himself on a large stone beside him. "Rise, and speak to me with freedom."

Mark rose, but turned his glowing face aside; he was ashamed to look at his companion.

"Sit down there," said Mr. Ewart, feeling for the boy's evident confusion and distress; "perhaps you are not yet aware that I have endeavoured to serve you—to procure you a situation with Farmer Joyce?"

"I have had it, and lost it," replied Mark abruptly.

"Indeed, I am sorry to hear that. I trust that no fault has occasioned your removal."

"I stole his fruit," said Mark, determined at least to hide nothing from his benefactor; "he turned me off, and he called me a hypocrite. I am bad enough," continued the boy, in an agitated tone; "no one but myself knows how bad; but I am *not* a hypocrite—I am *not!*"

"God forbid!" said Mr. Ewart; "but how did all this happen?"

"I was thirsty, it tempted me, and I took it. I broke all my resolutions, and now he cast me off, and you will cast me off, and the pure holy God, He will cast me off too! I shall never be worthy of heaven!"

"Did you think that you could ever be worthy of heaven?" said the clergyman, and paused for a reply. Then receiving none from Mark, he continued—"Not you, nor I, nor the holiest man that ever lived, One excepted, who was not only man, but God, was ever *worthy* of the kingdom of heaven."

Mark looked at him in silent surprise.

"We are all sinners, Mark; all polluted with guilt. Not one day passes in which our actions, our words, or our thoughts, would not make us lose all title to eternal life. The Bible says, ' *There is not one that doeth good, no, not one.*' Every living soul is included under sin."

"How can this be?" said Mark, who had looked upon the speaker as one above all temptation or stain.

"Since Adam, our first parent, sinned and fell, all his children have been born into the world with a nature tainted and full of wickedness. Even as every object lifted up from the earth, if unsupported, will fall to the ground, so we, without God's grace, naturally fall into sin."

"Then can no one go to heaven?" said Mark.

"Blessed be God, mercy has found a means by which even sinners can be saved! Sin is the burden which weighs us to the dust, which prevents us from rising to glory. The Lord Jesus came from heaven that He might free us from sin, take our burden from us, and bear it Himself; and so we have hope of salvation through Him."

"I wish that I understood this better," said Mark.

"I will tell you what happened to a friend of my own, which may help you to understand our position towards God, and the reason of the hope that is in us. I went some years ago with a wealthy nobleman to visit a prison at some distance. Many improvements have been made in prisons since then, at that time they were indeed most fearful abodes. In one damp dark cell, small and confined, where light scarcely struggled in through the narrow grating to show the horrors of the place, where the moisture trickled down the green stained walls, and the air felt heavy and unwholesome; in this miserable den we found an unhappy prisoner, who had been confined there for many weary years. He had been placed there for a debt which he was unable to pay, and he had no prospect of ever getting free. Can you see in this man's case no likeness to your own? Look on sin as a debt, a heavy debt, that you owe: do you not feel that you have no power to pay it?"

"None," replied Mark gloomily; "none."

"I had the will to help the poor man," continued Mr. Ewart, "but Providence had not afforded me the means. I had no more ability to set him free from prison than I have to rid you of the burden of your sin."

"But the wealthy nobleman," suggested Mark.

"He had both power and will. He paid the debt at once, and the prisoner was released. Never shall I forget the poor man's cry of delight, as the heavy iron-studded door was thrown open for his passage, and he bounded into the bright sunshine again!"

"And what became of him afterwards?" asked the boy.

"He entered the service of his generous benefactor, and became the most faithful, the most attached of servants. He remained in that place till he died; he seemed to think that he could never do enough for him who had restored him to freedom."

" Where is the friend to pay *my* debt?" sighed Mark.

" It has been paid already," said the clergyman.

" Paid!   Oh, when, and by whom?"

"It was paid when the Saviour died upon the cross —it was paid by the eternal Son of God.   He entered for us the prison of this world, He paid our debt with His own precious blood, He opened the gates of eternal life; through His merits, for His sake, we are pardoned and saved, if we have faith, true faith in that Saviour!"

"This is wonderful," said Mark, thoughtfully, as though he could yet scarcely grasp the idea.   "And this faith must produce a holy life; but here is the place where I went wrong—I thought men were saved *because* they were holy."

"They are holy because they are saved!   Here was indeed your mistake, my friend.   The poor debtor was not set free because he had served his benefactor, but he served him *because he was set free!*   A tree does not live because it has fruit, however abundant that fruit may be; but it produces fruit *because it has life*, and good actions are the fruit of our faith!"

" But are we safe whether we be holy or not?"

" *Without holiness no man shall see the Lord.   Every tree that beareth not good fruit is hewn down and cast into the fire.*"

" But I feel as if I could not be holy," cried Mark.

" I tried this day to walk straight on in the narrow

path of obedience to God—I tried, but I miserably failed. I gained nothing at all by trying."

"You gained the knowledge of your own weakness, my boy; you will trust less to your resolutions in future, and so God will bring good out of evil. And now let me ask you one question, Mark Dowley. When you determined to set out on your Christian pilgrimage, did you pray for the help and guidance of God's Spirit?"

Mark, in a low voice, answered, "No!"

"And can you wonder then that you failed? could you have expected to succeed? As well might you look for ripe fruit where the sun never shines, or for green grass to spring where the dew never falls, or for sails to be filled and the vessel move on when there is not a breath of air. Sun, dew, and wind are given by God alone, and so is the Holy Spirit, without which it is impossible to please Him."

"And how can I have the Spirit?" said Mark.

"Ask for it, never doubting but that it shall be sent, for this is the promise of the Lord: *Ask and ye shall receive, seek and ye shall find, knock and it shall be opened unto you. If ye, being evil, know how to give good gifts unto your children, how much more shall your Father which is in heaven give the Holy Spirit to them that ask him?*"

"And what will the Spirit do for me?"

"Strengthen you, increase your courage and your

faith, make your heart pure and holy. *The fruit of the Spirit is love, joy, peace, long-suffering, gentleness, goodness, faith, meekness, temperance.* Having these you are rich indeed, and may press on your way rejoicing to the kingdom of your Father in heaven."

"But how shall I pray?" exclaimed Mark. "I am afraid to address the Most High God, poor miserable sinner that I am."

"When the blessed Saviour dwelt upon earth, multitudes flocked around him. The poor diseased leper fell at his feet, he was not despised because he was unclean; parents brought their children to the Lord, they were not sent away because they were feeble; the thief asked for mercy on the cross, he was not rejected because he was a sinner. The same gentle Saviour who listened to them is ready to listen to you; the same merciful Lord who granted their prayers is ready to give an answer to yours. Pour out your whole heart, as you would to a friend; tell Him your wants, your weakness, your woe, and you never will seek Him in vain!"

There was silence for a few minutes, during which Mark remained buried in deep, earnest thought. The clergyman silently lifted up his heart to heaven for a blessing upon the words that had been spoken; then, rising from his seat, he said, "I do not give up all hope, Mark Dowley, of procuring a situation for you yet; though, of course, after what has occurred, I shall find it more difficult to do so. And one word before we part. You are now standing before the gate of mercy, a helpless, burdened, but not hopeless sinner. There is One ready, One willing to open to you, if you knock by sincere humble prayer. Go, then, without delay, *seek ye the Lord while he may be found, call ye upon him while he is near."*

Mark watched the receding figure of the clergyman with a heart too full to express thanks. As soon as Mr. Ewart was out of sight, once more the boy threw himself down on the grass, but no longer in a spirit of despair. Trying to realize the truth, that he was indeed in the presence of the Saviour of whom he had heard— that the same eye which regarded the penitent thief with compassion was now regarding him from heaven —he prayed, with the energy of one whose all is at stake, for pardon, for grace, for the Spirit of God! He rose with a feeling of comfort and relief, though the burden on his heart was not yet removed. He believed that the Lord was *gracious and long-suffering, that Jesus came into the world to save sinners;* he had knocked at the strait gate, which gives entrance into life, and mercy had opened it unto him!

CHAPTER V.

"Upon that place stood a Cross, and a little below, in the bottom, a Sepulchre. So I saw in my dream, that just as Christian came up with the Cross, his burden loosed from off his shoulders, and fell from off his back."—*Pilgrim's Progress.*

'ELL, this has been a pretty end to your fine pilgrimage!" cried Jack, as Mark, resolved to tell the truth, whatever it might cost him, finished the account of his rupture with the farmer.

"The end!" said Mark; "my pilgrimage is scarcely begun."

"It's a sort of backward travelling, I should say," laughed Jack. "You begin with quarrelling and stealing; I wonder what you'll come to at last?"

Mark was naturally of a quick and ardent spirit, only too ready to avenge insult, whether with his tongue or his hand. But at this moment his pride was subdued, he felt less inclined for angry retort; the young pilgrim was more on his guard; his first fall had taught him to walk carefully. Without replying, therefore, to the taunt of Jack, or continuing the subject at all, he turned to Ann Dowley, and asked her if she could lend him a needle and thread.

"What do you want with them?" asked Ann.

"Why, I am afraid that I shall be but a poor hand at the work, but I thought that I might manage to patch up one or two of these great holes, and make my dress look a little more respectable."

"And why do you wish to look respectable?" asked Madge, glancing at him through the uncombed, unwashed locks that hung loosely over her brow; "we get more when we look ragged."

"To-morrow is Sunday," Mark briefly replied, "and I am going to church."

"To church!" exclaimed every other voice in the cottage, in a tone of as much surprise as if he had said that he was going to prison. Except Ann, in better days, not one of the party had ever crossed the threshold of a church.

"Well, if ever!" exclaimed Jack; "why on earth do you go there?"

"I go because I think it right to do so, and because I think that it will help me on my way."

"And what will you do when you get there?" laughed Ben.

"I shall listen, learn, and pray."

Ann, who, by dint of searching in a most disorderly

box, filled with a variety of odds and ends, had drawn forth first thread and then needle, stretched out her hand towards Mark. " Give me your jacket, I will mend it," said she.

" Oh, thank you, how kind !" he cried, pulling it off, pleased with an offer as unexpected as it was unusual.

" I think," said Madge, " that the shirt wants mending worse than the jacket ; under that hole on the shoulder I can see the red mark quite plainly."

" Be silent, and don't talk nonsense !" cried Ann, impatiently.

The children glanced at each other, and were silent.

" Are you going to the near church by the wood ?" said Ann.

" No," replied Mark ; "I have two reasons for going to Marshdale, though it is six or seven miles off. I would rather not go where—where I am known ; and judging from the direction in which his carriage was driven, I think that I should have a better chance at Marshdale of hearing Mr. Ewart."

" Hearing whom ?" exclaimed Ann, almost dropping her work, whilst the blood rushed up to her face.

" Mr. Ewart, the clergyman who has been so kind, the tutor to Lord Fontonore."

" Lord Fontonore ! does he live here ?" cried Ann, almost trembling with excitement as she spoke.

" I do not know exactly where he lives. I should

think it some way off, as the carriage was put up at the inn. Did you ever see the clergyman, mother?"

"He used to visit at my last place," replied Ann, looking distressed.

"I think I've heard father talk about Lord Fontonore," said Madge.

"No, you never did," cried Ann, abruptly.

"But I'm sure of it," muttered Madge in a sullen tone.

"If you know the clergyman, that's good luck for us," said Ben. "I daresay that he'll give us money if we get up a good story about you; only he's precious sharp at finding one out. He wanted to pay us a visit."

"Don't bring him here; for any sake don't bring him here!" exclaimed Ann, looking quite alarmed. "You don't know the mischief, the ruin you would bring. I never wish to set eyes upon that man."

"I can imagine her feelings of pain," thought Mark, "by my own to-day, when I first saw the clergyman. There is something in the very look of a good man which seems like a reproach to us when we are so different."

The next morning, as Mark was dressing for church, he happily noticed, before he put on his jacket, the word *Pilgrim* chalked in large letters upon the back.

"This is a piece of Jack's mischief," he said to himself. "I am glad that it is something that can easily be set right—more glad still that I saw it in time. I will take no notice of this piece of ill-nature. I must learn to bear and forbear."

Mark endured in silence the taunts and jests of the children on his setting out on his long walk to church. He felt irritated and annoyed, but he had prayed for patience; and the consciousness that he was at least trying to do what was right seemed to give him a greater command over his temper. He was heartily glad, however, when he got out of hearing of mocking words and bursts of laughter, and soon had a sense even of pleasure as he walked over the sunny green fields.

At length Marshdale church came in view. An ancient building it was, with a low, ivy-covered tower, and a small arched porch before the entrance. It stood in a churchyard, which was embosomed in trees, and a large yew-tree, that had stood for many an age, threw its shadow over the lowly graves beneath.

A stream of people was slowly wending along the narrow gravel walk, while the bell rang a summons to prayer. There was the aged widow, leaning on her crutch, bending her feeble steps, perhaps for the last time, to the place where she had worshipped from a child; there the hardy peasant, in his clean smock-frock, leading his rosy-cheeked boy; and there walked the lady, leaning on her husband's arm, with a flock of little ones before her.

Mark stood beneath the yew-tree, half afraid to venture

further, watching the people as they went in. There were some others standing there also, perhaps waiting because a little early for the service, perhaps only idling near that door which they did not mean to enter. They were making observations on some one approaching.

" What a fine boy he looks! You might know him for a lord ! Does he stay long in the neighbourhood ?"

" Only for a few weeks longer, I believe; he has a prodi-

AT THE CHURCH.

gious estate somewhere, I hear, and generally lives there with his uncle."

As the speaker concluded, young Lord Fontonore passed before them, and his bright eye caught sight of

Mark Dowley. Leaving the path which led to the door, he was instantly at the side of the poor boy.

"You are coming into church, I hope?" said he earnestly; then continued, without stopping for a reply, "Mr. Ewart is to preach; you must not stay outside." Mark bowed his head, and followed into the church.

How heavenly to the weary-hearted boy sounded the music of the hymn, the many voices blended together in praise to the Saviour. God made him think of the harmony of heaven! Rude voices, unkind looks, quarrelling, falsehood, fierce temptations—all seemed to him shut out from that place, and a feeling of peace stole over his spirit, like a calm after a storm. He sat in a retired corner of the church, unnoticed and unobserved: it was as though the weary pilgrim had paused on the hot, dusty highway of life, to bathe his bruised feet in some cooling stream, and refresh himself by the wayside.

Presently Mr. Ewart ascended the pulpit with the Word of God in his hand. Mark fixed his earnest eyes upon the face of the preacher, and never removed them during the whole of the sermon. His was deep, solemn attention, such as befits a child of earth when listening to a message from Heaven.

The subject of the Christian minister's address was the sin of God's people in the wilderness, and the means by which mercy saved the guilty and dying. He described the scene so vividly that Mark could almost fancy that he saw Israel's hosts encamping in the desert around the tabernacle, over which hung a pillar of cloud, denoting the Lord's presence with his people. God had freed them from bondage, had saved them from their foes, had guided them, fed them, blessed them above all nations, and yet they rebelled and murmured against Him. Again and again they had broken His law, insulted His servant, and doubted His love; and at last the long-merited punishment came. Fiery serpents were sent into the camp, serpents whose bite was death, and the miserable sinners lay groaning and dying beneath the reptiles' venomous fangs.

"And are such serpents not amongst us still?" said the preacher; "is not *sin* the viper that clings to the soul, and brings it to misery and death! What ruins the drunkard's character and name, brings poverty and shame to his door? The fiery serpent of sin! What brings destruction on the murderer and the thief? The fiery serpent of sin! What fixes its poison even in the young child, what has wounded every soul that is born into the world? The fiery serpent of sin!"

Then the minister proceeded to tell how, at God's command, Moses raised on high a serpent made of brass, and whoever had faith to look on that serpent, recovered from his wound, and was healed. He described the trembling mothers of Israel lifting their children on high to look on the type of salvation; and the dying fixing upon it their dim, failing eyes, and finding life returning as they gazed !

" And has no such remedy been found for man, sinking under the punishment of sin ?   Thanks to redeeming love, that remedy has been found ; for as Moses lifted up the serpent in the wilderness, so hath the Son of Man been lifted up, that whoso believeth in him should not perish, but have everlasting life !   Behold the Saviour uplifted on the cross, His brow crowned with thorns, blood flowing from His side, and the wounds in His pierced hands and feet !   Why did He endure the torment and the shame, rude blows from the hands that His own power had formed—fierce taunts from the lips to which He had given breath.   It was that He might redeem us from sin and from death—it was that the blessed Jesus might have power to say, *Look unto Me and be ye saved, all ends of the earth.*

" We were sentenced to misery, sentenced to death ; the justice of God had pronounced the fearful words— *The soul that sinneth it shall die !*   One came forward who knew no sin, to bear the punishment due unto sin ; our sentence is blotted out by His blood ; the sword of justice has been sheathed in His breast; and now there is no condemnation to them that are in Christ Jesus ; their ransom is paid, their transgressions are forgiven for the sake of Him who loved and gave Himself for them.   Oh, come to the Saviour, ye weary and heavy laden—come to the Saviour, ye burdened with sin, dread no longer the wrath of an offended God ; *look to Him and be ye saved, all ye ends of the earth !*"

Mark had entered that church thoughtful and anxious, he left it with a heart overflowing with joy. It was as though sudden light had flashed upon darkness ; he felt as the cripple must have felt when given sudden strength, he sprang from the dust, and went walking, and leaping, and praising God. "No condemnation !" he kept repeating to himself, "no condemnation to the penitent sinner ! All washed away—all sin blotted out for ever by the blood of the crucified Lord ! Oh, now can I understand that blessed verse in Isaiah, '*Though your sins be as scarlet, they shall be white as snow; though they be red like crimson, they shall be as wool.*' '*Praise the Lord, O my soul! and all that is within me, praise His holy name!*'"

That hour was rich in blessings to the young pilgrim, and as he walked towards home, with a light step and lighter heart, it was his delight to count them over. He rejoiced in the free forgiveness of sins, which now for the first time he fully realized. He rejoiced that he might now appear before God, not clothed in the rags of his own imperfect works, but the spotless righteousness of his Redeemer. He rejoiced that the Lord had sealed him for His own, and given him sweet assurance of His pardon and His love. Oh, who can rejoice as the Christian rejoices when he looks to the cross and is healed !

CHAPTER VI.

THE PILGRIM IN HIS HOME.

" I saw then in my dream that he went on thus, even until he came to the bottom, where he saw, a little out of the way, three men fast asleep, with fetters upon their heels."—Pilgrim's Progress.

THE poor despised boy returned hungry and tired to a home where he was certain to meet with unkindness, where he knew that he would scarcely find the necessaries of life, and yet he returned with feelings that a monarch might have envied. The love of God was so shed abroad in his heart, that the sunshine seemed brighter, the earth looked more lovely ; he felt certain that his Lord would provide for him here, that every sorrow was leading to joy. He thought of the happiness of the man once possessed, when he sat *clothed and in his right mind* at the feet of the Saviour : it was there that the pilgrim was resting now, it was there that he had laid his burden down. The fruit of the Spirit is peace and joy, such joy as is the foretaste of heaven.

And the love of God must lead to love towards man. Mark could feel kindly towards all his fellow-creatures

His fervent desire was to do them some good, and let them share the happiness that he experienced. He thought of the rude inmates of his home, but without an emotion of anger; in that first hour of joy for pardoned sin there seemed no room in his heart for anything but love and compassion for those who were still in their blindness.

As Mark drew near to his cottage, he came to a piece of ground overgrown with thistles, which belonged to Farmer Joyce. He was surprised to find there Jack, Madge, and Ben pulling up the thistles most busily, with an energy which they seldom showed in anything but begging.

"Come and work with us," said Ben; "this ground must be all cleared to-day."

"And why to-day?" said Mark.

"Because Farmer Joyce told us this morning that when it was cleared he would give us half-a-crown."

"You can work to-morrow."

"Ah, but to-morrow is the fair-day, and that is why we are so anxious for the money."

"I will gladly rise early to help you to-morrow, but this day, Ben, we ought not to work. The Lord has commanded us to keep the Sabbath holy, and we never shall be losers by obeying Him."

"Here's the pilgrim come to preach," cried Madge in a mocking tone.

"I tell you what," said Jack, stopping a moment in his work, "you'd better mind your own business and be off; I don't know what you have to do with us."

"What I have to do with you!" exclaimed Mark. "Am I not your brother, the son of your mother? Am I not ready and willing to help you, and to rise early if I am ever so much tired?"

There was such a bright, kindly look on the pale, weary face, that even Jack could not possibly be offended.

"Now, just listen for a moment," continued Mark; "suppose that as I was coming along I had spied under the bushes there a lion asleep that I knew would soon wake, and prowl in search of his prey, should I do right in going home and taking care of myself, barring our door so that no lion could come in, and never telling you of the danger at all?"

Madge glanced half-frightened towards the bushes, but Jack replied, "I should say that you were a cowardly fellow if you did."

"What! leave us to be torn in pieces, and never give us warning of the lion?" cried Ben.

"I should be a cowardly fellow indeed, and a most unfeeling brother. And shall I not tell you of your danger, when the Evil One, who is as a roaring lion, is laying wait for your precious souls. As long as you are in sin you are in danger. Oh, that you would turn to God and be safe!"

"God will not punish poor children like us," said Madge, "just for working a little when we are so poor."

"The Evil One whispers the very same thing to us as he did to Eve, '*Thou shalt not surely die;*' but she found, as we shall find, that though God is merciful, He is also just, and keeps His word."

"There will be time enough to trouble ourselves about these things," said Ben.

"Take care of yourself, and leave us in peace!" exclaimed Jack; "we are not going to be taught by you!" and turning his back upon Mark, he began to work more vigorously than ever.

Mark walked up to the cottage with a slow, weary step, silently praying for those who would not listen to him. "God can touch their hearts though I cannot." thought he. "He who had mercy on me may have mercy on them."

Never had the cottage looked more untidy or uncomfortable, or Ann's face worn an expression more gloomy and ill-tempered.

"Mother," cried Mark cheerfully, "have you something to give me, my long walk has made me so hungry?"

"We've had dinner long ago."

"But have you nothing left for me?"

"You should have been here in proper time. It's all gone."

Exhausted in body, and wounded by unkindness,

Mark needed indeed the cordial of religion to prevent his spirit from sinking. But he thought of his Lord, and his sufferings upon earth. " My Saviour knew what it was to be weary and a hungered—He knew what it was to be despised and rejected. If He drained the cup of sorrow, shall I refuse to taste it! If this trial were not good for me, it would not be sent." So Mark sat down patiently in a corner of the room, and thought over the sermon to cheer him.

His attention was soon attracted by Ann's giving two or three heavy sighs, as if she were in pain; and looking up, he saw a frown of suffering on her face, as she bent down and touched her ankle with her hand.

" Have you hurt yourself, dear mother? " said he.

" Yes; I think that I sprained my ankle this morning. Dear me, how it has swelled! "

" I am so sorry! " cried Mark, instantly rising. " You should put up your foot, and not tire it by moving about. There," said he, sitting down at her feet, " rest it on my knee, and I will rub it gently. Is it not more easy now?"

Ann only replied by a sigh, but she let him go on, and patiently he sat there, chafing her ankle with his thin, weary fingers. He could scarcely prevent himself from falling asleep.

" That is very comfortable," said the woman at last; " certainly it's more than any of the others would do for their mother; they never so much as asked me how I did

MARK'S KINDNESS.

You're worth all the three, Mark," she added bitterly, "and little cause have you to show kindness to me. Just go to that cupboard—it hurts me to move—you'll find there some bread and cheese left."

Mark joyfully obeyed, and never was a feast more delicious than that humble meal. Never was a grace pronounced more from the depths of a grateful heart than that uttered by the poor peasant boy.

CHAPTER VII.

" Now, about the midway to the top of the hill was a pleasant arbour made by the Lord of the hill for the refreshment of weary travellers."— *Pilgrim's Progress.*

EVERAL days passed with but few events to mark them. Mark did everything for Ann to save her from exertion, and under his care her ankle became better. He also endeavoured to keep the cottage more tidy, and clear the little garden from weeds, remembering that " cleanliness is next to godliness," and that if *any man will not work, neither should he eat.*

One morning Madge burst into the cottage where Mark and Ann were sitting together. " He is coming !" she exclaimed in a breathless voice ; " he is coming—he is just at the gate ! "

" Who ? " cried Ann and Mark at once.

" The parson—the—"

" Not Mr. Ewart ! " exclaimed Ann, starting up in terror.

"Yes it is—the tall man dressed in black."

In a moment the woman rushed to the back room as fast as her ankle would let her. "I'll keep quiet here," she said. "If he asks for me, say that I have just gone to the miller's."

"Mother's precious afraid of a parson," said Madge, as a low knock was heard at the door.

With pleasure Mark opened to his benefactor.

"Good morning," said Mr. Ewart, as he crossed the threshold. "I have not forgotten my promise to you, my friend. I hope that I have obtained a place for you as errand-boy to a grocer. Being myself only a temporary resident in these parts, I do not know much of your future master, except that he appears to keep a respectable shop, and is very regular in attendance at church; but I hear that he bears a high character. Mr. Lowe, if you suit him, agrees to give you board and lodging; and if he finds you upon trial useful and active, he will add a little salary at the end of the year."

"I am very thankful to you, sir," said Mark, his eyes expressing much more than his lips could. "I trust that you never will have cause to be sorry for your kindness."

"Is your mother within?" said Mr. Ewart.

Mark bit his lip, and knew not what to reply, divided between fear of much displeasing his parent, and that of telling a falsehood to his benefactor.

"She's gone to the miller's," said Madge boldly.

But the clergyman turned away from the wicked little girl, whose word he never thought of trusting, and repeated his question to Mark, whose hesitation he could not avoid seeing.

"She is within, sir," said the boy, after a little pause; then continued with a painful effort, as he could not but feel that Ann's conduct appeared rude and ungrateful to one whom above all men he was anxious to please; "but she would rather not see you to-day."

"Very well, I have seen you; you will tell her what I have arranged." Mark ventured to glance at the speaker, and saw, with a feeling of relief, that Mr. Ewart's face did not look at all angry.

It was more than could be said for Ann's, as, after the clergyman's departure, she came out of her hiding-place again. Her face was flushed, her manner excited; and, in a fit of ungovernable passion, she twice struck the unresisting boy.

"Lord Jesus, this I suffer for thee!" thought Mark; and this reflection took the bitterness from the trial. He was only thankful that he had been enabled to keep to the truth, and not swerve from the narrow path.

On the following day Mark went to his new master, who lived in a neighbouring town. He found out the shop of Mr. Lowe without difficulty; and there was something of comfort and respectability in the appearance of the establishment that was very encouraging to the boy. To his unaccustomed eye the ranges of shining brown canisters, each neatly labelled with its contents; the white sugar-loaves, with prices ticketed in the window; the large cards, with advertisements of sauces and soap, and the Malaga raisins, spread temptingly to view, spake of endless plenty and abundance.

Mark carried a note which Mr. Ewart had given to him, and, entering the shop, placed it modestly on the counter before Mr. Lowe.

The grocer was rather an elderly man, with a bald head, and mild expression of face. He opened the note slowly, then looked at Mark over his spectacles, read the contents, then took another survey of the boy. Mark's heart beat fast, he was so anxious not to be rejected.

"So," said Mr. Lowe, in a slow, soft voice, as if he measured every word that he spoke, "so you are the lad that is to come here upon trial, recommended by the Reverend Mr. Ewart. He says that you've not been well brought up; that's bad, very bad—but that he hopes that your own principles are good. Mr. Ewart is a pious man, a very zealous minister, and I am glad to aid him in works of charity like this. If you're pious, all's right, there's nothing like that; I will have none about me but those who are decidedly pious!"

Mr. Lowe looked as though he expected a reply, which

puzzled Mark exceedingly, as he had no idea of turning piety to worldly advantage, or professing religion to help him to a place. He stood uneasily twisting his cap in his hand, and was much relieved when, a customer coming in, Lowe handed him over to his shopman.

Radley, the assistant, was a neat-looking little man, very precise and formal in his manner, at least in the presence of his master. There was certainly an occasional twinkle in his eye, which made Mark, who was very observant, suspect that he was rather fonder of fun than might beseem the shopman of the solemn Mr. Lowe; but his manner, in general, was a sort of copy of his master's, and he borrowed his language and phrases.

And now, fairly received into the service of the grocer, Mark seemed to have entered upon a life of comparative comfort. Mr. Lowe was neither tyrannical nor harsh, nor was Radley disposed to bully the errand-boy. Mark's obliging manner, great intelligence, and readiness to work, made him rather a favourite with both, and the common comforts of life which he now enjoyed appeared as luxuries to him.

"I have been climbing a steep hill of difficulty," thought he, "and now I have reached a place of rest. How good is the Lord, to provide for me thus, with those who are his servants!"

That those with whom Mark lived were indeed God's servants, he at first never thought of doubting. Was

there not a missionary-box placed upon the counter—
was not Mr. Lowe ever speaking of religion—was he
not foremost in every good work of charity—did he not
most constantly attend church ?

But there were several things which soon made the
boy waver a little in his opinion. He could not help
observing that his employer took care to lose no grain
of praise for anything that he did. Instead of his left
hand not knowing the good deeds of his right, it was no
fault of his if all the world did not know them. Then,
his manner a little varied with the character of his
customers. With clergymen, or with those whom he
considered religious, his voice became still softer, his
manner more meek. Mark could not help suspecting
that he was not quite sincere. The boy reproached
himself, however, for daring to judge another, and that
one so much more advanced in the Christian life than
himself. He thought that it must be his own inexperi-
ence in religion that made him doubt its reality in
Lowe.

Thus a few weeks passed in comfort with Mark ; but
the pilgrim was making no progress. It is not well for
us to dwell amongst those whose profession is greater
than their practice. The fervour of Mark's first love
was a little cooled. Alas ! in weak, infirm mortals, such
as we are, how inclined is that fervour to cool ! There
were no strong temptations to stir up the flame—no

anxious fears to drive him to the mercy-seat—his prayers were perhaps more frequent, but they were less deep and earnest. Mark was tempted to rest a little upon forms, and think that all must be right, because others approved.

The Christian must not dream that he is only in danger whilst dwelling with the careless or profane. The society of professors may be quite as dangerous, by lulling his conscience to sleep. He is less on his guard against inward foes, less able to distinguish true religion in his heart, from the natural desire to please, and many of God's children on earth have found the arbour more dangerous than the hill!

Not that Mark did much with which he could reproach himself, unless it were that he never sought an opportunity of going to see his mother. He connected nothing but ideas of persecution and unkindness with his home. He thought that by this time John Dowley might have returned, a man who had ever treated him with unnatural cruelty; and to say the truth, Mark rather dreaded going again near the place. I fear that my pilgrim is falling in the estimation of my reader; but I am drawing no sinless model of perfection; and, perhaps, if we closely examine our own hearts, even after they have been enlightened by the Spirit, there may be something in our own experience which will remind us of this chapter of the life of the pilgrim. I said that Mark suspected a little the sincerity of the religious professions of his master. This suspicion was painfully strengthened by an incident which occurred when he had been a few weeks under his roof.

One night, after the shop had been closed, and prayers said, and Mark had retired to his small attic, he fancied that he heard a little noise down below, and crept from his chamber to listen. All was very still, only the clock on the stairs seemed to tick twice as loudly as usual. Then again there was a slight sound, apparently from the shop, and Mark wondered what, at that hour, it could be. Softly he crept down the creaking stair, unwilling to disturb his master, who had retired to rest rather earlier than usual, happening to feel not very well. Mark reached the door which opened into the shop, and there was no doubt left that somebody was within engaged in some occupation.

Mark observed that the door, though nearly closed, was not shut, a narrow line of light showed it to be a little ajar; he pushed it very gently to widen the opening, and within, to his surprise, saw Radley.

"Who's there?" exclaimed the shopman; "why, Mark, is it you? That's lucky, you'll come and help me, I daresay. I am so sleepy to-night—but this must be done."

"What are you doing?" said Mark, with a feeling of curiosity.

"I'm mixing this with that, as you see," replied Radley, pointing to two heaps of what looked like coffee on the counter.

MARK'S INDIGNATION AT DECEIT.

"Why should you mix them?"

"Oh, ask no questions, and I'll tell you no stories!" said Radley, quite dropping his usual formal manner, with a laughing look in his eye which startled the boy.

"Do you mean—is it possible—" exclaimed Mark, his face flushing with indignation as he spoke, "that you are mixing chicory with coffee in order to deceive our master's customers?"

"You are very green, or you would know that it is constantly done."

"It cannot be right," said Mark, "to sell an article under a false name, and get a false price for it too! Surely Mr. Lowe does not know what you are doing!"

"Oh, you most simple of simpletons!" laughed Radley; "do you suppose that I am doing it for my own diversion, to serve my pious master against his will?"

"You do it by his orders then?"

"Of course I do."

"I could never have believed that he could have been guilty of such a thing!" exclaimed Mark, more shocked and disgusted by the hypocrisy of Lowe, than by any of the open wickedness that he had ever witnessed. "And you, Radley, how can your conscience let you do what is so wrong?"

"My conscience is my master's, I only obey what he commands."

"Your conscience your master's! Oh no!" exclaimed Mark; "you will have to answer for yourself before God."

"If I refused to do this I should have to leave the grocer's service."

"Better leave his service than the service of God."

"I say, young man," replied Radley, still good-humouredly, though with some appearance of scorn, "mind your own business, and leave me to mind mine. When you carry the goods to the customers, no one asks you whether the parcel holds tea or gooseberry leaves."

"But can you endure to kneel down, and repeat prayers to the Almighty, when you know—"

"I tell you," said Radley, as though he thought it a joke, "my master's religion and mine is like the articles in this shop, it is mixed. But what matter? it makes as good a show as any, it serves our purpose, and I really think that the world likes to be taken in. We get on, look respectable, and thrive; what can be better than that?"

"Better to starve—better to struggle up hill all one's life, beset with difficulties and trials."

"We'll leave the starving to you, if you like it; and as for struggling up hill, only fools do that, if they can find an easier way round! Now go to your bed, and rest quiet my lad, and leave me and my conscience to settle our affairs together."

Startled as from a dream, Mark returned to his attic, disappointed, disgusted, and grieved. "Can a blessing ever rest on this house?" thought he; "can Lowe ever, even in this world, be really a gainer by such awful hypocrisy and deceit? Oh, I have been too little on my guard in this place, I have been a drowsy pilgrim on the way—blessed be God that I am awakened before too late!"

CHAPTER VIII.

DANGERS, DIFFICULTIES, AND DOUBTS.

" Fear not the lions, for they are chained, and are placed there for trial of faith where it is ; and for the discovery of those that have none : keep in the midst of the path, and no hurt shall come unto thee."—Pilgrim's Progress.

IT was long before Mark could get to sleep, and he awoke almost before it was light. He felt a heavy oppression which was new to him, and rose to open the window. The sky was now of that deep exquisite blue which it wears the hour before dawn ; the few stars that studded the heavens were growing pale at the approach of morning. The street was perfectly quiet, not a vehicle was moving about, and the sleepy sound of a cock crowing at some distance was the only noise that broke the stillness.

"I feel as though I could not rest," said Mark, "the sun will rise before long ; I will dress myself and go out, and have a quiet time before I am required to work. I have been keeping too little watch over myself lately, I have been too easily contented with the little knowledge to which I have attained. Oh, what if I should have been deceiving myself all the time—if I have never entered the strait gate at all!" Mark had lost for a time that sweet assurance which had afforded him such joy amidst trials.

Putting his Bible in his bosom that he might read it as he walked, Mark opened the door of his attic. The instant that he did so he became sensible of a most powerful smell of fire, and the next moment a volume of smoke came rolling up from below!

Mark sprang down the staircase with anxious haste, every step making him more certain of the fearful fact that the house of his master was on fire! He rushed first to the sleeping apartment of Radley, then roused up the servant of the house, and bidding her throw up the window and call loudly for assistance, hurried to the bedroom of Mr. Lowe.

Startled from deep sleep, hardly able to comprehend what had happened, only with a terrible consciousness that it was something dreadful, the wretched man rose from his pillow, and was half dragged by Mark from his apartment, which being immediately over the place of the fire, was becoming very hot, and full of smoke. Such an awakening is terrible here—but oh, what will it be to the hypocrite hereafter, when the trumpet of the angel shall rouse him from his grave to behold a uni-verse in flames!

Assistance was speedily given; the cry of "fire!" brought crowds of neighbours around; pails of water were passed from hand to hand, and the fire-engine soon came rattling up the street. The cries and shouts, the crackling and roaring of the devouring element, the suffocating dense clouds, through which little could be seen but tongues of fierce flame, now darting curling round the wood-work, now streaming upwards and reddening the black canopy of smoke—the stifling heat, the occasional glimpse of burning rafters, which looked as if glowing red hot in the fire, all formed a scene which time could never efface from the memory of those who beheld it!

Half wild with terror, anxiety, and grief, Lowe pushed his way here and there through the crowd, sometimes urging on the firemen, sometimes trying to assist them, sometimes standing still, to witness in helpless misery the destruction of his property. Well might he look on in misery, for that property was his *all!* The hypocrite had not laid up his treasure in heaven, and he now beheld, consuming before his eyes, that for which he had been daily bartering his soul!

Before the sun had reached his mid-day height, the fire had been entirely subdued. The efforts of the firemen had prevented it from spreading, but a charred and blackened shell of a house, floors, rafters, windows, all entirely destroyed, alone remained of the habitation of Lowe!

The unhappy man was offered shelter in the house of a sympathizing neighbour, and thither Mark went to see him. He found him in a pitiable state, his mind almost crushed by his misfortune, yet still, true to his character, he professed submission to the decree of Providence, even while his excessive grief showed how little he felt it, and intermixed his lamentations with various texts, thereby edifying his neighbours, perhaps, but shocking one who knew him better than they did.

He received his errand-boy with great kindness. " One of the most bitter parts of my trial," said the really kind-hearted though unprincipled man, " is that my ruin will throw you and poor Radley upon the world. I suppose that you will return home directly."

" I thought that I would go first to Mr. Ewart, and ask his advice."

" I grieve to say that will no longer be in your power. That excellent minister was to leave Marshdale for Yorkshire yesterday."

This piece of information fell like a heavy blow upon Mark, and his face showed how much he felt it. "Then I must return to the cottage at once," said he, in a low tone.

" I can understand your reluctance, my boy, to become a burden upon your poor parents."

There was not a particle of hypocrisy in Mark; he wanted no praise for motives which were not his. " I was not thinking about that," said he.

"Ah! I understand," said Lowe, in his own peculiar tone; "you feel being deprived of the spiritual advantages which you enjoyed while under my roof."

"Not exactly that," replied Mark, hesitating and looking embarrassed, for there was a mixture of this regret in his reluctance to return home, though it was not his principal feeling.

The truth was, that Mark dreaded not so much the poverty and discomfort of Ann's cottage—though he did not like that—as the positive cruelty which he would probably have to endure if he returned. Having for some time slipped his neck from the yoke, he shrank exceedingly from having to bear it again. A soldier who fights bravely on the battle-field, if he leave it for a while till his blood cools and his wounds begin to stiffen and smart, finds it a much greater trial of courage to return to his post than to stay there without ever quitting it.

But Mark seemed to have no other resource, and bidding a friendly farewell to his late master, who, whatever he was in the sight of Heaven, had ever been kind to him, he walked slowly up the street. The gloomy, threatening clouds above him, seemed like types of his darkened fate, and the forerunners of a storm. As he proceeded, pondering over the difficulties of his position, he was startled by the sight of a lady, who was standing at a door at which she had just knocked. Mark

had seen her but once before, but her face was imprinted
on a memory naturally good, especially as the most important event of his life, his repentance and turning to
God, was in some way connected with her.   She was
the lady who had dropped the bag by the stile which
contained Mark's precious Bible.

Now, it had often weighed upon the conscience of the
boy, that his dearest possession was not his by right;
and that if ever he met with its lawful owner, common
honesty bound him to restore it.   And yet, to give that
away which had been his life—to walk on in darkness,
without that light which had been his comfort and solace
till now—Mark felt almost as though he could not do
it, and stood hesitating and arguing in his own mind
till the lady entered the house, and the door closed
behind her.

"She is rich, she can buy many others," whispered
the Tempter in his bosom.   "She is certain to have
supplied its loss long ago; but you, where will you find
another?   You will lose all your religion with your
Bible, and fall under the temptations which you will be
certain to meet."   Was not this *mistrust* of God's
sustaining power?   "And what disgrace," added the
Tempter, "will it be to own taking and using that which
was not yours!   Notwithstanding your care, the book
has been injured; it is not worth returning to a lady.
She may question you about the other things in the

bag—the purse, the money, the handkerchief with lace ; of course you cannot betray your family ; you will be looked upon, perhaps punished, as a thief!" These were the suggestions of a *timorous* spirit, magnifying every danger by the way.

But against all this was the plain word of God, *Thou shalt not steal.* To keep anything from its owner that might be restored, was clearly to break the commandment. So, after a short inward prayer for the help which he so much needed, with a heart so low, and a frame so much exhausted by the excitement and fatigue of the morning, that it would have been a relief to him to have sat down and cried, Mark gently rang the bell.

He felt embarrassed when the servant-maid opened the door, and inquired what it was that he wanted. But, recovering himself, he asked if he might speak with the lady who had just entered the house. He said that he had something which he believed that she had lost ; and the servant, without making any difficulty, ushered him into the parlour.

A silver-haired old gentleman and the lady were there ; she had just opened a piano, and was sitting down to play. Her face looked so gentle and bright that Mark was somewhat reassured, though most reluctant to part with his treasure.

"What did you want with me, my good boy," said

MARK RESTORING THE LOST BIBLE.

the lady, turning round without quitting her seat, her fingers resting on the silent notes of the instrument.

Mark drew from his bosom the Bible. "I believe, ma'am, that this is yours," said he.

"My long-lost Bible!" exclaimed the lady, rising with an expression of joy. "Oh! I never thought to see it again. Where could you have found it?"

"Near a stile, where you had dropped it as you went to church."

"It was in my bag with other things; have you anything else?"

"I have nothing else," replied Mark, feeling very uneasy.

"What is your name?" said the old gentleman, looking up from his paper.

"Mark Dowley, sir," answered the boy.

"Mark Dowley! Ellen, have we not heard that name before?"

"Oh yes; 'tis the name of the boy in whom dear Mr. Ewart was interested. Do you not remember his speaking about him?"

"I remember it perfectly well, my dear; it is easy to imagine what became of the other contents of the bag."

"And where are you staying now?" said Ellen, with a look of interest; "I hope that you have a good situation."

"I had a good situation last night, but the fire that happened to-day burned down the house of my master, and now I am abroad in the world."

Ellen glided to her father, and whispered something in his ear. Mark's heart beat very quickly, he scarcely

knew why; but it was with a sensation of hope.
After a few minutes of conversation which he could not
hear, Mr. Searle—for that was the gentleman's name—
said aloud, "As you please, my dear; we certainly were
looking out for such a boy. We could take him with us
to Yorkshire; there could be no difficulty about that."

"Would you like," said Ellen, bending her kind eyes
upon Mark, "to become one of our household, to accompany us to Silvermere? Your work would be light,
and your situation comfortable. We live scarcely two
miles from Castle Fontonore."

With a rebound of joy all the greater from the depth
of his late depression, Mark eagerly accepted the offer.
Profiting, however, by the remembrance of past regrets,
and desirous to be more faithful to his duty in future,
he added that he must first obtain the consent of his
mother.

"You are quite right, my boy," said Mr. Searle,
kindly; "let nothing ever come between you and your
duty to a parent. Her will, next to God's, should be
your law; you never can do too much for her."

"But it is not desirable to go till to-morrow," said
Ellen; "those heavy clouds have burst; only see how
it rains! The poor boy looks quite knocked up already; he could occupy the little room here to-night."

This arrangement was finally concluded upon, and the
weary but thankful boy again found a haven of rest.

A comfortable meal was set before him, to which he was inclined to do full justice. He enjoyed deep untroubled sleep that night, and awoke in the morning refreshed and rejoicing. How the difficulties that he feared had melted away before him! How one painful effort made had brought its own rich reward!

CHAPTER IX.

" Then did Christian begin to be afraid, and to cast in his mind whether to go back or to stand his ground."—*Pilgrim's Progress.*

UR Pilgrim rose early, with a heart full of hope. He determined not to quit the house till he had seen Mr. Searle or his daughter again, and waited in the hall till they should come down. Mark's attention was at once riveted by what he had never seen before—a complete suit of armour hung against the wall; and while he was looking at it, and admiring its various parts, the master of the house approached him unobserved.

"That is a fine suit of armour," said Mr. Searle, " such as was worn in the time of the Crusades, when warlike pilgrims went to the Holy Land. Perhaps you have never heard of such ? "

" Yes, sir," replied Mark, modestly.

" There is the helmet, you see, to protect the head ; the mail to cover the body and breast ; the weighty sword, and the pointed shield. You observe the red cross upon it?"

The looks of Mark showed the interest that he took.

"We're not done with fighting yet," said the old gentleman, in a quaint manner which was peculiar to him. "While our three old enemies—the world, the flesh, and the devil—are lying in ambush to attack us, and the Holy Land which we hope to gain is before us, we must be armed pilgrims, ay, and fighting pilgrims too!"

"Pray go on, sir," said Mark, as the old gentleman stopped; "I so like to hear of these things."

"You see that our Leader has not sent us into battle unprovided. We have the Helmet of Proof, the Hope of Salvation, to prevent sinful doubts from wounding the head. Then the Breastplate of Righteousness to guard us; for we may be full of knowledge, and quite correct in our belief, but if we give way to wilful sin, of what avail is the soundness of the head when the heart is pierced by the fiery dart? Nor must we neglect the Girdle of Truth, nor the preparation of the Gospel of Peace for our feet."

"That is a part of the armour which I do not understand," said Mark.

"No? Long before you are as old as I, I hope that you will experimentally understand it. Yet I should think that you had known already what it is to tread some of the rough ways of life."

Mark heartily assented to this.

"And every one knows the difference between walk-ing with shoes and without them.   Were I barefoot, I should start if I trod on a thorn, I should bleed if I struck against a sharp-edged stone; and so it is with the people of this world who are not shod with the Preparation of Peace.   I have known the smallest thing worry and fret them; they were as wretched from one small brier in their path, as if it had been one labyrinth of thorns."

"And are all Christians safe from these little vexations?"

"I can't say that," replied the old gentleman, "I can't say that.   There are many who cannot tread down small difficulties, but go on their whole way to heaven shrinking and starting at the least of them.   But it strikes me that is because, while they have put on all the rest of the armour of God, they have neglected the sandals for the feet.

"Well, to proceed with our description of the armoury of heaven—We come next to the most wonderful, the most powerful of weapons—the Sword of the Spirit, which is the Word of God.   Now this flashed so bright, and its edge was so sharp, in the days of early Chris-tianity, that many were its conquests in various parts of the world, and old idolatry fell fast before it.   But when the great Enemy found that it could not be withstood, he devised a deep-laid scheme to destroy its effect, and made a curious sheath, all covered with jewels and gold; and the name of this sheath was Superstition. In this, for many ages, was the Word of God buried; and though flashes of its brightness shone out here and there, it was almost quite hidden from the eyes of the people, till Wickliffe, and Luther, and many Reformers beside— some yielding up their blood and their lives for the truth—drew it from its fatal scabbard, clear and glittering again ; and it sent forth a flash at its unsheathing that was seen over almost all Europe, and enlightened the distant shores of the New World.

"And now the last thing that we come to is the strong shield Faith. Without this neither helmet nor breastplate could have power to resist the shafts of the Enemy. St. Peter threw it aside in a moment of fear, and instantly his righteousness was pierced through and through. And it is not only in battle that our faith is precious ; we pillow our head upon it when we rest, and when we take water from the wells of salvation, it is in the hollow of this shield alone that we can raise it to our thirsting lips."

Ellen now came down-stairs, with her Bible in her hand ; that Bible which Mark had prized so dearly, and parted with so very unwillingly.

"I could not have the heart to deprive you of this," said she ; "take it, and keep it, and may you ever find it to be your best comforter and guide."

With what grateful joy Mark replaced the Bible in his bosom, and with what a courageous heart, about an hour after, he set forth to ask his mother's consent to remaining with Mr. Searle! He had very little doubt of obtaining it, or he would hardly have advanced with such a light, joyous step. When he had quitted the town, and found himself on the open plain, he gave vent to his happy emotions in songs of praise. We are commanded in everything to give thanks; let us never forget to do so when all seems smiling around us; no— and even when mists fall, and tempests gather over our heads, let us still remember in *everything* to give thanks.

How many thoughts were awakened in the Pilgrim's mind, as again he approached his home! There was the stile where the Bible had been found; there the stone upon which he had sat to read it, and felt such terror flash upon his mind at the words, "*The soul that sinneth, it shall die;*" there was the piece of ground which the children had been weeding, when he warned them, but vainly, to flee from the wrath to come. There was not a thistle now left on the spot; and as he looked at the earth, all cleared and prepared for seed, Mark silently prayed that the grace of God might likewise so prepare and make ready the hearts of his own little sister and brothers. He could see over the fields, at a little distance, the old ruin where he had first met Mr. Ewart;

not a day had passed, since that meeting, in which Mark had not prayed with grateful affection for him whose words had been such a blessing to his soul.

And now Mark stood at the door of the cottage; a loud, coarse voice which he heard from within announced to him, before he reached it, that John Dowley had returned. There were other things to show that a change had taken place, of which Mark became aware as he entered the cottage. A large pewter pot stood at the door, a black bottle and dirty pack of cards appeared on the table, a joint of meat was roasting before the fire, and Ann, who started with surprise on seeing him, wore a silk shawl and golden ear-rings. John must have returned with his pockets full of money.

He was sitting at the table, a short, stout-built man, with a louring expression in his bleared eye, and a face flushed by intemperance; no one who beheld them together would have imagined him to be the father of the pale, thoughtful, intellectual boy, to whose greeting he returned no answer but something resembling a growl. Mark fancied that Ann looked sorry to see him; but that, perhaps, was no sign of unkindness. Jack, Madge, and Ben, sprang eagerly forward, full of news, and of things to show him.

"See, Mark, what father has brought me!"

"We're getting so rich now!"

"Look at my brooch and my bracelets!"

Such were the sort of exclamations which, uttered all together, took the place of any words of welcome.

Mark, in his secret heart, thanked Heaven that it was not his lot to remain in this place.

"Sit down, Mark," said Ann, looking joyless, notwithstanding her finery; "and be silent, you children, will you? One can't hear one's own voice, in the midst of so much noise."

The children might not have obeyed their mother very readily, had not a savage look from John seconded her words.

"I thought that you had a good situation, Mark," continued the woman; "you've not been so foolish as to leave it?"

"You have not heard, then, of the fire which took place yesterday: poor Mr. Lowe has been burned out of house and home. But a far better situation has been offered to me. If you consent, and if father approve, I shall go to Yorkshire next week, with—"

"Yorkshire!" muttered John; "and what's the gentleman's name?"

"Searle; he lives at a place called Silvermere."

"Silvermere!" exclaimed both Dowley and his wife at once. Anne added, in a voice that was scarcely audible, "That's close to Castle Fontonore!"

"Everything is arranged for me," continued Mark; "but I thought that it would not be right to go so far without coming and asking your consent."

"Consent!" thundered Dowley, in a tone so loud that the cottage rang again, and the astonished children shrank closer to each other in fear. "Do you think that I ever would consent to *your* going *there?*"

Here was a blow so sudden, so unexpected, that it almost took away Mark's breath. Recovering himself soon, however, he began, "I should be able to maintain myself, perhaps even to assist—"

"Don't say one word more, or—" John uttered a horrible oath, but left his hearers to imagine, from his clenched hand and savage look, what was the threat which he intended should follow.

"At least," said Mark, in an agitated voice, "allow me to return and tell Mr. Searle that you forbid me to go with him. He would think me so ungrateful—"

"What do I care what he thinks!"

"Oh, is it not enough," cried Mark, in bitterness of spirit, "that my way is barred, that my hopes are ruined—" he could not speak on, his heart was too full.

"If he isn't going to cry!" whispered Jack.

"A pretty pilgrim, to be so soft!" murmured Ben.

These mocking words roused the spirit of the persecuted boy, but it was rather an earthly spirit of indignation than a spirit of endurance for the Lord's sake.

"Let him go," said Anne, "and tell the gentleman that he can't serve him; he can just say that you've found something better for him."

" He won't return if I once let him go."

" Yes, he'll return; won't you, Mark ? "

" Yes, I will," replied the boy, with difficulty restrain-
ing his tears at even so slight a mark of kindness.
John gave ungracious permission rather by silence than
words, and Mark left the cottage almost choking with
his feelings.

It was a little time before he could regain sufficient
composure even to look his difficulties in the face.   Oh,
it is hard to go down into the deep Valley of Humiliation, and few are those called upon suddenly to descend
from their high hopes but meet with some slips by the
way!

Mark was tempted, and this was a grievous temptation, to doubt even God's goodness and mercy towards
him.   Why was he placed in a situation so painful,
why suddenly plunged back into that furnace of trial
from which he had so lately been snatched?   It seemed
to Mark as if the Almighty had forsaken him, as if God
had forgotten to be gracious, and had left a poor mortal
to be tempted beyond what he could bear!

The pilgrims to heaven must expect on their way
thither to meet sometimes with trials like this.   The
Evil One whom they served in the days of their ignorance
will not suffer a victim to escape him, without making
efforts—strong and subtle efforts too—to draw back the
ransomed soul to his service.   He put rebellious thoughts

into the mind of Mark, like so many fiery darts, to make him chafe with an impatient and despairing spirit, under the difficulty of obeying the fifth commandment; and which of us dare say that in such an inward struggle we should have stood our ground better than he?

But Mark had not been so lately warned and armed, to make no fight against his Enemy. He had still power to lift up his heart in prayer; to try to recall some precious promise on which to stay his sinking spirit. *"Lo, I am with you alway, even unto the end,"* was the word from Scripture with which he now met the Enemy. The Saviour whom he loved was beside him here, the Saviour was witnessing his struggle with sin, would help him, would bless him, if his faith failed not. Oh, better that wretched abode with the presence of his Lord, than the stateliest palace without it! Could he who had been forgiven so much, could he who had been promised so much, faint in the moment of trial! Where should the soldier be but in the battle— what should a pilgrim do but bear his cross!

With thoughts like these poor Mark was struggling for submission, and resisting the suggestions of evil; but the tempter had yet another shaft in his quiver, and tried by arousing another passion to crush down the resistance of piety and conscience. Mark heard a quick step behind him, felt a heavy hand on his shoulder, and turning round beheld John Dowley.

"You walk fast," said the man; "I could hardly overtake you. You were going to the town, were you not? well, I've a little job for you to do for me there."

Mark signified how readily he would do it.

"You see these two bright sovereigns," said the man, taking two yellow pieces from a heavily filled purse, and putting them into the hand of the boy. "I want these changed—you understand me; buy some trifle at two different shops—mark me, two shops not too near each other; and bring back the change in silver."

"What trifles do you want?" said Mark, poising the coins upon his finger.

"Anything—gingerbread, or sugar-plums, if you like; only see that the change is right."

Mark struck the two pieces against one another; he did so again, as if not satisfied with the sound. "Are you sure that these are good?" said he.

"What does that matter to you? put them in your pocket, and do as I bid you."

"Forgive me," replied the boy; "but I dare not."

"Dare not! I did not know that you were such a coward. What are you afraid of—the police?"

"I fear doing wrong; I fear offending my God. Oh, father, I *cannot* pass that money."

"Say that word again," muttered Dowley between his teeth, raising a cudgel that he grasped in his hand.

"Ask anything else—anything that is not wrong!

I consented for you to give up my place. I obeyed you, though in sorrow and disappointment ; but this thing I may not, cannot do, even if refusing cost me my life !"

" Then take the consequences !" exclaimed the man in a fury of passion, seizing the unhappy boy with one hand, while with the other he showered on him a torrent of blows. Mark winced beneath them, struggled, called out for assistance; but neither fear nor torture made him lift a hand against his earthly oppressor, or yield to the assault of the tempter within, who urged him to procure mercy at the price of his conscience !

Wearied at length with his barbarous labour, Dowley flung his bruised, bleeding, gasping victim into a dry ditch, and muttering to himself that he had served him out at last, walked with long, hurried strides from the spot.

CHAPTER X.

" Now at the end of this valley was another, called the Valley of the
Shadow of Death."—*Pilgrim's Progress.*

"H! this is fearful : this is more terrible than all!"
muttered Mark, as he regained slowly the consciousness that he had half lost. He attempted
to raise himself, but motion was torture. He
called out, but no one answered to his cry;
he had been crossing the fields by a shorter path than
the highroad, and therefore was not in the direct line of
any thoroughfare, and might lie there for hours unnoticed.
Mark felt as though the Shadow of Death were upon
him; his mind was too confused and dizzy for prayer;
it seemed to grasp nothing but the consciousness that
something horrible had occurred. For long he lay
there, half delirious with pain. The Pilgrim was passing
through, perhaps, the darkest passage of his life.

How different was the fate of young Lord Fontonore,
as, with his tutor seated beside him in his splendid carriage, he rolled along the highroad towards the north !

"1 am so glad that yesterday's storm is over!" cried he. "There's nothing like travelling in an open carriage, except when it pours as it did last night. It raises one's spirits, passing fast through the air, when the horses dash on without touch from the whip; and the air is so fresh, and the sky so blue, and every turn of the wheel brings us nearer to home!"

"Then you are not sorry to return to the castle?"

"Sorry! oh no! I am too fond of it, too proud of it, for that! I shall be glad, too, to see the old faces again; Aunt Matilda, pretty Clemmy, my uncle, and all. I hope that I shall find my pony all right. I shall enjoy a good gallop again! Oh, I shall be delighted to see my own home with the drawbridge, and the moat, and the old yew hedge; and the flag will wave on the tower, I know, on my return, to welcome the little master back! Then we must go to see my tenants, especially old Widow Grove; I am impatient to take her the shell ornament which I have bought for her: and my poor dear old friend who lives at the mill—what a welcome 1 shall have from him! Oh, my tenants will not be sorry to have me amongst them again! And yet," rattled on the lively boy, "I have enjoyed myself exceedingly here. How I delighted in our visit to that old ruin; don't I see it there, just beyond the fields? Now, Mr. Ewart, I have something to remind me of everything but that; just let me stop the coachman," he continued, drawing the check-string, "and run off for one stone."

"I think, Charles, that we have a long journey before us; it is hardly desirable to delay."

"Oh, but I'll not be two minutes, you'll see. I'll be back again, like the lightning!" and, without waiting for the steps to be let down, he sprang lightly out of the carriage.

"Heaven bless the dear boy!" inwardly prayed Mr. Ewart, as he saw the graceful form bounding away. "Heaven bless him, and make him a blessing to many! A noble career seems to be before him, and he has a kind, a noble, a generous heart, which has already, I trust, been given to God. But I fear for him, the dangers of his position; he will have so much to nourish pride; and pride, alas! is his besetting sin. His guardian, and his aunt, rather foster than check it; and London, to which he is to be taken in the winter, will be full of snares to the young peer. But why should I thus take anxious thought? I earnestly strive to impress on his heart the truths of our holy religion. He is willing to listen, and ready to learn; can I doubt that a blessing will rest on my prayerful efforts, or that he who is ever a Father to the orphan, will guard my dear pupil in the hour of temptation?"

The clergyman was suddenly arrested in his meditations by a loud call from Lord Fontonore, who had reached the other end of the field; and looking in that direction, he saw the boy waving his hat, and making impatient and excited gestures as if to entreat him to come to him. Convinced that no trifle thus moved his pupil, Mr. Ewart instantly descended from the carriage,

MARK DISCOVERED BY LORD FONTONORE.

and ordering the man-servant to follow, proceeded rapidly towards the spot.

"Oh, sir! oh, Mr. Ewart, only look here!" exclaimed Charles, as soon as his tutor came within hearing. "Poor

Mark Dowley, only see how they have treated him. He is not dying—oh, I trust that he is not dying!"

"Help me to raise him," said the minister quietly, though his blood ran cold at the spectacle before him. "Do you not think, Charles, that you could find a little water?" The boy was off almost before the sentence was concluded. "Jones, we must draw off his jacket very gently,—softly, you pain him; we must examine his hurts."

With a hand gentle as a woman's, Mr. Ewart removed the garment from the half senseless sufferer, to stanch the blood, and ascertain the amount of his injuries. But he had scarcely laid bare the poor bruised shoulders of the boy, when he started with an expression of such extreme surprise that Jones looked in wonder to see what could be its cause.

"Is it possible!" exclaimed the clergyman, "can it be really so! Yes, for the countenance confirms it, so like the mother; it struck me the first moment that I saw him! And the woman—ah!" he cried, pressing his hand on his forehead, "I remember she would not see me; she dared not, the base—the treacherous! It must be so; I see all now—but the motive, what could be the motive!"

"Please, sir," said Jones, touching his hat, "shall I go to yonder cottage for assistance?"

"Carry the boy to the carriage;—no, I will bear him

myself; it is not the first time that he has been in my arms
And listen, Jones, say not a word of what we have found,
but seek out two or three stout labourers at once ; the
police would be better, but we must not lose time, everything depends upon secrecy and despatch."

While the wondering servant went in search of the
required aid, Mr. Ewart, with feelings almost resembling
those of a father, after binding with his own handkerchief
and neckcloth Mark's most severe wounds, gently carried
him to where the carriage stood waiting. Once the poor
boy unclosed his eyes, and uttered an exclamation of
pleasure on recognizing the clergyman, but he seemed
almost too feeble to speak. Mr. Ewart had scarcely
reached the high road when he was joined by Lord
Fontonore, who, flushed and panting in the eagerness of
his haste, brought some cold water in his cap.

" Go back with him, Charles, to the house which we
have just left, and call upon the surgeon in your way.
Oh, be tender with him, as if he were your brother !"
the clergyman's voice trembled as he spoke.

" And you—"

" I have a sterner duty to perform, but it is one of
the utmost importance. There, support the poor fellow's
head on your breast, you see that the water has made him
revive; all will be right yet, by the blessing of Heaven!"

As the carriage was turned round, and driven rapidly
towards Marshdale, Jones came up with two powerful-

looking ploughmen, and almost at the same time Mr. Searle, who was walking along the road, reached the spot where they were now standing together.

"Most opportunely met!" cried the minister, grasping his hand; "you are a magistrate, you will go with us, and lend sanction to our proceedings." He drew the old gentleman aside, and whispered rapidly a few sentences in his ear, at which the watchful Jones observed that Mr. Searle looked surprised and shocked. Then, turning towards the three, "Follow me, my men," said Mr. Ewart, abruptly; "a great crime has been committed, we go to seize the criminals." And without giving any further explanation, he led them rapidly towards the cottage of Dowley.

If Dowley felt any remorse for the barbarous manner in which he had treated Mark, he was now occupied in drowning all memory and feeling in that fiery drink which ruins so many souls. He had even filled the cups of his children with spirits, and the cottage was a scene of wild, unholy mirth, such as might make the pure angels weep. The sudden entrance of Mr. Ewart without knock or previous warning, a grave, stern expression on that usually mild face, startled the party as though he had been an apparition. He fixed his piercing eye upon Ann, who shrank back and covered her face with her hands, then turned it full upon Dowley whose flushed face showed mingled emotions of anger and fear.

"I think that I have seen you before," said the clergyman; "is not your name John Lawless? were you not once gamekeeper to Lord Fontonore?"

"That's not my name, nor never was," replied the man surlily; "and I never heard of Lord Fontonore in my life."

"What! not from your wife there, who was nurse in the family, and intrusted with the charge of the eldest son?"

"I say, what," exclaimed the man, starting up furiously, "I don't know what brings you here, forcing yourself into a man's home without his leave; you shall go out a little quicker than you came—"

"Ay, but I shall not go alone," replied Mr. Ewart, striking the table with his hand. At the signal, in rushed Jones and the two countrymen, followed by the magistrate; and after a short but furious struggle, they succeeded in securing their prisoner.

Ann attempted to make her escape by the back-door; Mr. Ewart laid his hand upon her arm.

"You are our prisoner also," he said, "unhappy woman! nothing remains to you now but to make all the reparation in your power, by a frank and full confession."

Ann wrung her hands in despair.

"What is to be done with the children?" said Mr. Ewart to the magistrate, looking round on the frightened, miserable family.

"Their proper home is the workhouse—I will see to them ; and these prisoners must be sent to the jail."

The clergyman gazed on the children with strong compassion. "We must consider if nothing better can be done for them," thought he. "Poor inheritors of misery in this world, Heaven grant that they may have been taken from evil influence in time to preserve them, through God's grace, from misery in that which is to come !"

CHAPTER XI.

"Looking forward, he saw Faithful before him upon his journey."
Pilgrim's Progress.

 FEW hours afterwards, as Charles was sitting in his own room, amusing himself with his pencil, he was joined by his tutor, who looked weary and pale, as if suffering from exertion and excitement.

"I hope that you have found out who beat the poor boy so cruelly, and have given him up to justice," exclaimed Charles.

"The man whom I suspect is in custody," replied the clergyman, sinking wearily down on a chair. "I find that Mark is asleep; 'tis the best thing for him."

"Yes, poor fellow, he has been sleeping for the last hour. The surgeon is to call again in the evening. But you look exceedingly tired, dear sir; let me bring you a glass of wine."

"No, Charles, thank you; it is not wine that I require. I am full of anxious thought, my dear boy." And he passed his hand across his pale forehead.

" Anxious thought for Mark ?" inquired Charles.

" No; rather anxious thought concerning you."

" Well, that's odd," said the boy, looking at him with a surprised smile; "you seemed pretty easy about me in the morning, and I assure you that I have been most harmlessly employed since you were away, first looking after Mark, and then drawing a plan of a church."

" Let me see it," said the clergyman, holding out his hand.

" Oh, it is not finished, so you must make allowance," replied Charles, looking at his own performance, however, with no dissatisfied air. " I shall very probably make plenty of alterations and improvements, as it will be more than nine years before I can carry out my plans; but I've such a glorious design in my head—something that I will do when I come of age and have my own money !"

Charles was too much engrossed with his project to notice the grave, almost sad, expression on the features of his tutor; so he ran on in his animated manner,—

" You know what a long way my village is from the church, and how seldom the clergyman can visit my poor people. Well, I am determined to build a church of my own, a large, handsome church, with the sittings all free; and you shall be the clergyman, my own dear Mr. Ewart, and live in the Castle with me all my life ! Do you not approve of my plan ?" added the boy, looking into his face with a bright smile.

" Man proposes, God disposes," said Mr. Ewart, laying his hand affectionately upon the shoulder of his pupil.

Charles felt disappointed. " I thought that you would have been so much pleased," cried he ; " I am sure that you wish me to try to serve the Lord."

" Most assuredly," replied the clergyman ; " but the Lord himself will choose out the way in which we are to serve him. Do you remember the young man who came to our Saviour, and asked him what he should do to inherit eternal life ? "

" Ah ! the one who went away sorrowing, because he had great possessions."

" I have little doubt," said Mr. Ewart, " that had he been commanded to build a place of worship, or to give liberal alms, he would at once have willingly complied."

" But he was told to give up *all !* Do you know, sir, that it has often struck me that that was a command very hard to obey. I am glad that in these days there is no need for such commands."

" There is the same need now, Charles, that there was then for a spirit of willing obedience. We may not now be called upon to give up all, but every Christian must be *ready* to do so. If there is anything on earth on which we fix our hearts, so as to say, *I can yield to God anything but this*, that thing from that moment is an idol and a snare, and we are breaking the second commandment."

8

Charles was silent for a few moments, thinking over his tutor's words, till Mr. Ewart began conversation on a different subject.

" You must sometimes have heard speak of an infant brother of your own."

" Oh yes, little Ernest, who was drowned three days before I was born, whose marble monument I so constantly see in church—a lovely baby, sleeping amongst water-lilies."

" His monument is there, but not his body."

" No, poor little one, it never was found. I have heard all about his death many a time: how his careless nurse set him down to crawl on the grass, and was either called away or fell asleep, I forget which, and the poor baby rolled into the river and was lost, nothing of him being recovered but his little hat and plume, which was found floating on the top of the water."

" That was the story which was told at the time by one who shrank not from adding falsehood to cruelty."

" And the nurse was half wild with grief, and dared not wait till the return of her master, who had gone to London with my poor mother on account of her health; but she soon ran away, no one knew whither, and never could be traced any more."

" She fled the place," said Mr. Ewart, " with a man who became her husband—one who, for his bad conduct, had been dismissed by your father from the office of gamekeeper, with a threat to send him into jail. This wicked man never forgot or forgave the threat, and tempted the wretched woman whom he made his wife to a crime, in order to gratify his revenge. The babe was *not* drowned, but stolen. After much ill-treatment and cruelty from the unprincipled pair, who brought him up as their own son, his true birth was at length providentially discovered by the clergyman who had baptized him more than twelve years before, from a most singular mark on his shoulder."

" You cannot mean Mark !" exclaimed Charles, in extreme surprise.

" I do mean Mark ; the confession of Ann has con-firmed my suspicions. I have not the shadow of a doubt that the boy is your brother."

It was strange to watch the various emotions fast succeeding one another on the handsome countenance of Charles—astonishment, interest, doubt, pity, succeeded by a grave, inquiring look, as he said, " Then, if Mark be my brother, who is Lord Fontonore ?"

" He is, as the eldest son of your late father."

The face of Charles fell. " Then what am I ?" said he

" Charles Hope ; the same as your uncle."

" And the estate, and the castle, with its fine old hall, and all the pictures, everything that I have so prized and looked on as my own—are they all his ?"

" Everything is entailed on the eldest son."

"And have I nothing?" exclaimed Charles, his man-ner becoming excited; "what is to become of me, then?"

"You will enter some profession, my dear boy, as your uncle did, and earn your livelihood honourably, I trust."

"But I am only a boy; how am I to be supported till then?"

"Doubtless either something will be allowed from the property of your brother, or your uncle will—"

"Oh, I can't stand this!" exclaimed Charles, passion-ately, springing from his seat, and walking up and down the room in a state of excitement. "To be dependent —that is more than I can bear! It is bad enough to be poor, but to be dependent!"

"Oh, my almost son!" exclaimed the clergyman, with emotion, "does not this very excess of grief at its loss prove that what is taken away would have been a snare to you? May you not reckon in another world amongst your chief mercies that which is now so painful to bear?"

"And all my schemes of usefulness, too!" cried Charles, flinging himself down again upon his chair.

"None can say what a career of usefulness may be before you yet. You may more glorify God, and more benefit man, than had your efforts never been stimulated by the necessity for exertion."

"If Mark had been the younger brother, it would

have been far better; he would have been more than contented, and I—"

"Let us never, Charles," said Mr. Ewart, laying his hand upon his shoulder, " say that anything which man

CHARLES'S STRUGGLE.

had no power to alter could be better than as the Almighty ordained it. Could we see all that He sees, past and future together; could we know all that He knows, both our powers and our interests, we should not even wish such things other than as they are ; we should feel that whatever is, is right."

But pride, arrogance, and love of worldly glory were speaking too loudly in the heart of Charles to suffer him yet to listen quietly to the voice of truth. "I little thought when I found Mark what I was bringing upon myself," said he ; "and you, sir," he added, bitterly, " you have thought much more of your new friend than of your old."

Unjust as was the reproach, it wounded Mr. Ewart. "What would you have had me do, Charles?" he said sadly, but without anger. "Gross wrong had been done, I could set it right ; a much-injured boy had been long kept from his birth-right, would you have had me join with his oppressors in depriving him of it?"

Charles was silent, but felt ashamed of his own injustice.

"At present you and I are alone in possession of the secret. Ann's confession was made only to me ; would you wish me, were the matter in your own choice, to hush up the affair, let all things go on as before, and leave you to enjoy—not enjoy, but possess—the title and estate, which is the right of a brother?"

"Oh no ; I am not quite so wicked as that!" cried Charles, throwing himself into the arms of his friend, and burying his face in his bosom. "Forgive me ! oh, forgive me my impatience and injustice ! You were right ; the things which it pains me so to part with, I was not fit to keep. They must have been my idols, though I did not know it. But this trial seems to have made me full of evil."

" It has not made the evil, it has only shown it to you, my dear boy. Water often looks clear until it is stirred ; but the stirring does not cause the sand which arises, it was there while the water looked purest."

" This, then, is one of the uses of trial, I suppose, to make us know how wicked we are. An hour ago I felt so good and so happy, I thought the way to heaven so easy and delightful ; and in the very first difficulty that I met, all my goodness melted away in a moment."

" But now that you are recalled to yourself—now that you remember that as strangers and pilgrims upon earth, we must not cling too closely to anything in a world through which we are but passing—I trust that, by God's help, you will show how cheerfully a Christian can submit to the will of his Master. You will not go away, like the rich young man, sorrowing, but, following the Saviour through all life's changing scenes, rejoice in the treasure laid up for you in heaven."

" One thing I should like," said Charles, his face brightening again, " may I be the first to tell the news to Mark ? If he is half as much delighted as I was vexed—I should so like to see how he takes it ! "

"Most readily do I accede to your wish," said Mr.
Ewart, "but we must say nothing to excite him just
now, while he is so feverish; and it is better that he
should know nothing of the change until all is more
decided and settled. I am just going to write to your
uncle."

"My uncle!" said Charles, looking again rather grave;
"ah, how astonished he will be, and Aunt Matilda, and
Clementina! I wonder if it will make them feel differently towards me—if I shall lose many friends with
my title."

"There is one at least whom you will gain."

"Ah, a brother! I daresay that Mark and I will
love each other, only I can never fancy him a lord."
Charles almost laughed at the idea.

"You must be to him what Jonathan was to David.
One might have feared that the son of King Saul, who
must naturally have once hoped to succeed to the throne
of his father, would have beheld with jealousy the shepherd boy who was chosen to rule in his stead. Yet
between the two there was only confidence and love, love
which, however much we may admire it in David, appears tenfold more beautiful in his friend."

"We must be like Christian and Faithful in the Pilgrim's Progress," said Charles, now quite regaining his
usual cheerfulness of manner. "He has been passing
through the Valley of the Shadow of Death, and strug-

gling under all manner of trials, and now the way is growing smooth beneath his feet, and he will have a brother to walk beside him. He will teach me something of the Valley of Humility, and I will tell him what I know of Vanity Fair. I feel really ashamed of myself now—what a worldly, self-seeking pilgrim I have been ! "

"God be praised ! " murmured the clergyman, as he quitted the room ; "God be praised, who has supported and strengthened my dear pupil in the hour of his sore temptation."

CHAPTER XII.

PILGRIM'S CONVERSE BY THE WAY.

" I have sowed, and you have reaped; and the day is coming when ' both he that soweth and they that reap shall rejoice together:' that is, if you hold out; ' for in due season ye shall reap, if ye faint not.' "—*Pilgrim's Progress.*

 FEW days after, as Mr. Ewart entered the room in which Mark, or rather Ernest, as we must now call him, was sitting in an arm-chair, propped up by cushions, and looking exceedingly pale, Charles, who was looking over the back of the chair, addressed his tutor playfully with the words, "I am so much disappointed, Mr. Ewart; here's a young nobleman to whom I have been telling all sorts of good news, and he looks as grave as a judge upon them all."

"I feel so bewildered," said Ernest, pressing his pale brow; "I think that it must all be a dream."

"It is no dream," said Mr. Ewart, seating himself by his side; "all is true that your brother has told you."

"Brother!" exclaimed Ernest, fixing his moistened eyes upon Charles, "Oh, my lord!"

"He is so wilful," laughed Charles; "we shall never get him to sign himself Fontonore."

"I do not wish to be a lord," said Ernest, gravely; "I am not fit to be a lord. I know next to nothing. I have hardly read a book but the Bible. Oh, do you be the nobleman, and let me be your brother! You shall have the fortune, and the estates, and all that—I never could bear to deprive you of them!"

"You have no choice, Ernest," said Mr. Ewart; "you can no more help being a noble than you can help being your father's son : you cannot avoid receiving the ten talents ; your care now must be to make a right use of them. Both Ann and Lawless have publicly confessed."

"I hope that they are not to suffer on account of me," said Ernest; "especially my mo— she whom I once thought my mother. It would imbitter the whole of my life."

"Lawless is committed to trial for forgery (a purse of base coin was found on his person); Ann, for her conduct towards you. I will try to do all in my power, as it is your wish, to make the sentence of the law fall lightly on the woman."

"And my brothers?" said Ernest.

"What of me?" interrupted Charles. "Oh, I see that you intend to disown me already," he added, playfully; "you will neither believe nor acknowledge me, so I shall leave you to the management of Mr. Ewart," and so saying he left the apartment.

"I am going to ask what I fear you will think a strange question," said Ernest to the clergyman, as soon as they were alone; "I know that I am to have a very large fortune, but—but—shall I have any of it to spend as I like now?"

"You will doubtless have the same allowance that has been given to Charles," replied Mr. Ewart, naming the sum.

"So much!" exclaimed Ernest in surprise; "and Lord Fontonore—I mean my brother?"

"What he may receive will depend upon his uncle. Poor Charles! he has nothing of his own."

"Half of mine at least shall be his. Let him have it without knowing from whom it comes."

Mr. Ewart smiled, and pressed the boy's hand.

"And those unhappy children with whom I have been brought up, now separated from their parents, and helpless and friendless—tell me, sir, what can I do for them?"

"There are some excellent charities in London, where such are received, brought up to an honest trade, and instructed in the principles of religion. But there is considerable expense in keeping children at such asylums, unless they have been admitted by votes, which in the present case would be very difficult to procure."

" Would the remaining half of my allowance be
enough ? "

" You would leave yourself nothing, my dear boy. I
honour your motives and feelings, but generosity must
be tempered by prudence. The little girl you might
place at an asylum."

" And the boys ? "

" Let me think what could be done with them. It
seems to me," said the clergyman, after a minute's consideration, " that Mr. Hope might allow them, if such
were really your desire, to be brought up under the
gardener at the castle."

" That is an excellent plan ! " cried Ernest, clapping
his hands ; " there they would always be under your
eye ; you would teach them also the narrow way to
heaven ! "

" There might be some objections to the plan," said
Mr. Ewart, reflecting ; " it might place you uncomfort-
ably to have those near the castle who had known you
in such a different position."

" It will be good for me," said Ernest, with animation. " If I ever am tempted to be lifted up with pride,
I shall have but to look at them and remember what I
was ; and if anything can humble me, that will. Will
you kindly write to Mr. Hope directly ? "

" There is no need to do that," replied the clergyman ;
" I have heard from him to-day, and came now to tell

you that it is his wish that as soon as you are equal to moving, you and your brother should start at once for the castle."

"Oh, I am ready for anything!" cried Ernest; "I mean that I am ready to travel," he added, correcting himself, "for my new situation I fear that I am not ready."

"The two best introductions to any new sphere of life are—trust in God, and mistrust of ourselves."

"Do you think that I shall have many dangers now, I mean as a pilgrim?" asked Ernest.

"You will have dangers still, though of a different kind. Your battle-field is changed, but not your enemy. The good seed in your heart was in peril before from the hot sun of trial beating upon it; now God grant that the cares, riches, and pleasures of this world may not spring up as thorns to choke it! Your great refuge must be self-examination and prayer; with these, by God's grace, you will safely walk still on the slippery high path before you."

"I trust that nothing will make me forget that I am a pilgrim," said Ernest.

"I will give you this book, which I look upon as a valuable chart of the way you must tread," replied Mr. Ewart, placing in the hand of Ernest a copy of Bunyan's Pilgrim's Progress. "In this book you will see the Christian's path, over part of which you yourself have travelled.

You will recognize some spots that are familiar to you, some people with whom you have had to deal; and you will see, as if a curtain were drawn up before you, much that you are likely to meet with in the future."

" Oh, thanks! this must indeed be a most wonderful book! But I cannot understand how it can tell me about things that have happened or will happen to myself, the paths of people through life are so many."

" The paths of men are many—the Christian has but one. Our circumstances, indeed, are very various; to some the hill Difficulty comes through bitter poverty, to some from unkind relations, to some from broken health. Some pass through the gloomy valley in sunshine, and see but little of its horrors; some are helped, some hindered on their way to heaven by those amongst whom they live. But there are certain points in the pilgrimage which *every* Christian must know. We *all* set out from the City of Destruction—we are all by nature born in sin. Even children must flee from the wrath to come, turning from—that is, repenting of their unrighteousness. Even children must come to the one strait gate—faith in our Lord Jesus Christ; must knock by prayer, and having once entered in, must press on in the way leading unto life! Even children bear a burden of sin, though the sooner they come to the cross of the Saviour the lighter that burden must be ; but were it only the burden of one unholy *word*, one sinful *thought*, nothing but the blood of the Lord Jesus Christ could take even that away! Even children are beset by spiritual foes—must, if pilgrims, know something of the battle within; even children must wear the whole armour of God; and to the youngest, the weakest, is offered the crown which the Lord has prepared for them that love Him!"

"What a wonderfully wise and learned man he must have been who wrote such a book as you say that this is!"

"It was written by a man who had very little learning except what he gained from the Word of God itself. The wisdom which he possessed came from above, and the men of the world deemed it foolishness. The author of that book was a tinker, named Bunyan, a man who supported himself by the labour of his hands, and who for twelve years, only on account of his religion, was confined in Bedford jail."

"Were men put in prison for being religious?" exclaimed Ernest, in surprise.

"At all times the world has been an enemy to holiness, and religion has been liable to persecution; but this persecution has at different times taken very different shapes. The early Christians were tortured, beaten, thrown to wild beasts, till so many people had adopted their holy faith that the civilized world began to call itself Christian. Then the Evil One, seeing that he could not put out the light, heaped up a thousand superstitions around it, so that sinners might be prevented from seeing it. Yet, doubtless, even through the dark ages, as they are called, God had always some faithful believers upon earth, whom the world would hate because they were not of it; and persecute, though not always openly. At length the time of the Reformation arrived; brave men and holy forced a way through the mass of superstitions which had hidden the precious light of truth; and then, indeed, there was a fearful struggle, and persecution bathed its sword in the blood of martyrs. Many were the stakes raised in England, Germany, and France, where saints yielded up their souls in the midst of flames. But no persecution could tread out the light which God himself had kindled. As blows upon gold but make it spread wider, so the very efforts of the wicked to suppress the truth, made it more extensively known."

"And was it then that Bunyan was imprisoned?"

"Not then, but more than a century after, in the reign of an unworthy monarch, Charles II., when the light which had shone so brightly was becoming obscured again by superstition and worldly policy. Bunyan was confined for preaching the Word; was separated from the family of whom he was the support. That which most deeply wounded his heart was the helpless position of his poor blind child, who so much needed the protecting care of a father."

"And they imprisoned him for twelve years? How cruel! What a tedious, weary trial it must have been to him!"

"God honoured the prisoner far above the prince; He made the jail a nobler dwelling than a palace! It was there that the despised and persecuted tinker composed his wonderful book. Bright, holy thoughts were his pleasant companions. While his worldly judges were passing through life, surrounded by cares, business, and amusements, seeing, perhaps, nothing beyond this fleeting scene, the prisoner was tracing the Pilgrim's Progress, copying from his own heart the Pilgrim's feelings, noting from his own life the Pilgrim's trials, and describing from his own hopes the Pilgrim's reward. And when his book was finished—when, with humble faith, he laid it as an offering before Him who had given him the power to write it—how little could the despised Bunyan have anticipated the honour which God would put upon that book! It has been read by thousands and hundreds of thousands—generation after generation have delighted in it—the high and the low, the rich and the poor, all have welcomed the chart of the Pilgrim. It has been translated into many foreign tongues; from east to west, from north to south, in all the four quarters of the globe, it has directed sinners to the one strait gate, and guided them along the one narrow path. I believe," added Mr. Ewart, laying his hand upon the volume, "that next to the Bible, *from which it is taken,* that this book has been the most widely circulated of any ever written; and never shall we know, till the last great day, how many a saved and rejoicing spirit may trace its first step in the heavenward way to reading Bunyan's Pilgrim's Progress."

CHAPTER XIII.

"Then I saw in my dream, that when they were got out of the wilderness, they presently saw a town before them, and the name of that town
is Vanity."—*Pilgrim's Progress.*

"H ! what a strange remembrance I shall always
have of that old ruin !" exclaimed Charles,
as again he drove past the well-known spot,
in a carriage with post-horses, on his way
to Castle Fontonore. But this time he had
another companion beside him ; Ernest, well wrapped up
in cloak and furs—for the autumn was now advanced—
was resting on the soft cushions of the luxurious vehicle.

"What will your remembrances be, compared to
mine?" said Ernest, raising himself to look out, and
keeping his eyes fixed upon the gray pile until it was
lost to his sight.

" I went to pick up a stone as a keepsake, and I found
a brother !" cried Charles.

" How much I owe you !" said Ernest, fervently. " I
make you an ill return by taking away what you thought

your birthright! And you, sir," he added, turning towards the clergyman, "my debt to you I can never never repay; but my heart's gratitude and love shall be yours as long as I breathe. All the honours and riches that I possess I value as nothing, compared with the blessing of having such a friend and such a brother."

This was the first time that Ernest had been able to express so much; for, shy and retiring as he was by nature, and rendered more so by the manner in which all the warm feelings of his heart had hitherto been chilled and repressed, he had wrapped himself up in a cloak of reserve, and had few words to show how deep were these feelings. Mr. Ewart saw that in the boy's present weak state he was easily agitated and excited, and, to change the subject of a conversation which made Ernest's voice tremble with emotion, asked him how he liked the book which he had given him.

"I find it very interesting. I should have thought it so, if I had only read it as an amusing story; but what you said about its showing us things that happen in our own lives, has made it a thousand times more so. I could enter into so many of the feelings of Christian—his misery with his burden, his delight when it rolled away. I am almost sure that Mr. Worldly Wiseman once turned me aside, and I fancy that I have even known a little of the Slough of Despond!"

"The earlier children go on pilgrimage, the less they

usually know of the misery of that slough. As Bunyan, in his allegory, beautifully represents, there are stepping-stones across it all the way, and the feet of Christ's little ones usually find these, so that many have reached the wicket-gate in safety, without one stain of the slough on their garments."

"What a mercy it was to Christian to meet with Evangelist! Sir, you have been Evangelist to me."

"And I must be your Faithful," said Charles, smiling.

"Oh no! for then I should lose you in Vanity Fair," replied Ernest, looking fondly on his brother, who was daily becoming dearer to his heart.

"Vanity Fair is not at all like what it was when Bunyan wrote," said Charles. "There is no danger of my being put in prison, or stoned, or burned, because I may not like the ways of the place; so you are not in the least likely to lose me in that manner, and I may be your Faithful and your Hopeful both in one."

"Is Vanity Fair quite done away with now?" said Ernest to Mr. Ewart.

"No, my boy, and never will be, as long as the three grand tempters of the world, *the lust of the flesh, the lust of the eye, and the pride of life,* spread their attractive stalls to lure unwary pilgrims."

"I am afraid that you will think me a very dull pupil," said Ernest; "but I do not exactly understand who these tempters are of whom you speak."

"The lust of the flesh is pleasure; the lust of the eye, covetousness; the pride of life is that fatal pride, whether of birth, riches, talent, or beauty, which is often viewed with indulgence by the world, but which is particularly hateful to God."

"But must all pleasure be sinful?" asked Charles.

"By no means. Some pleasure springs directly from religion. Of heavenly wisdom it is written in God's Word, *Her ways are ways of pleasantness, and all her paths are peace.* And other pleasure may be hallowed by religion; but it must be pleasure that has no connection with *sin.* We may gather life's flowers, but we must be careful that they are those which have not the trail of the serpent upon them."

"Is it wrong to enjoy the riches which God gives us?" asked Ernest. "Shall I sin if I look with joy on the noble estate and all the beautiful things which you tell me are mine?"

"God forbid," replied the clergyman; "hath He not *given us all things richly to enjoy?* But we must *use the world as not abusing it.* There is a test by which we can easily find out if riches are not clogging and delaying us in our heavenward path. We must examine, *first,* if we receive them with gratitude, as coming from God; "*secondly,* if we are watchful to spend them to the glory of God; "*thirdly,* if we are ready to resign them, in obedience to God."

"I think," observed Charles, "that Ernest will be less in danger from the pride of life than I was."

"Yes," said Ernest, looking admiringly at his brother; "because I shall have so very much less to be proud of."

"I never meant that," cried Charles, colouring; "but I fancy that you have been so tried and subdued, by suffering so much, that you will never be so foolish and flighty as I; you will not be so easily puffed up."

"I am sure that I could not answer for myself," replied Ernest, simply.

"No; and certainly you are very ignorant of the ways of Vanity Fair; that's the part of your pilgrimage that you are coming to now."

"Surely not till I go to London. I shall see nothing of it while we stay quietly studying at the castle."

"Little you know!" exclaimed Charles, laughing. "My good Aunt Matilda, my pretty little cousin, and perhaps my business-like uncle himself, may introduce you—" Charles stopped, for he caught his tutor's eye, and its grave expression silenced him at once.

"*Judge not, that ye be not judged,*" said the clergyman, impressively. "There is nothing so little becoming a young pilgrim as passing unkind judgment on his elders."

"I'm afraid that it's my besetting sin," said Charles, "and one that it is very difficult to get rid of."

" Like many others, I believe that it springs from pride," observed his tutor. " When we are deeply sensible of our own imperfections, we have more mercy to show, or less attention to give to those of our neighbours and companions."

The journey to Yorkshire took two days, travelling by post being so much slower than by railway. To Ernest they were days of almost unmixed delight : change of scene, unaccustomed comforts, the society of those whom he loved, all the hopes which naturally gild the prospect of youth—all the brighter for being so new —filled his cup of enjoyment very full. Though his manner was not so lively as that of his brother, it was easy to see that his happiness was not less.

We may be surprised that the bitter emotions which Charles had entertained when he first knew of the loss of his title seemed so soon to have entirely disappeared. But his was an open and generous heart—Ernest's sufferings had roused his pity—his brother's grateful affection had flattered his feelings—he was pleased with himself for his conquest over pride ; and perhaps nothing tends to make us more cheerful than this. Then there had been nothing to make him painfully aware of a change —his tutor's manner had been more kind than ever— Jones could never address him but as " my lord "— Ernest seemed unwilling to consider himself even as his equal—all his comforts appeared the same as ever.

It was therefore with unaffected pleasure that, as they approached near the Castle Fontonore, Charles pointed out the landmarks to his brother.

"There now, there's the lodge ; isn't it a beauty? That's Widow Grove who is standing at the gate. Why, there's quite a little crowd ; I knew that there would be one.   Take off your cap, Ernest, they are cheering for us.   Did you ever see such magnificent timber in your life? so glorious with the autumn tints still upon them ! That tree to the right is five hundred years old.   Just look at the deer as they bound through that glade ; and now—yes—now you have a glimpse of the castle, and there's the flag waving from the top of the tower.   Is it not an inheritance worth having, Ernest?   Does it not surpass your expectations?"

"It does, it does ; I never saw, never dreamed of anything so beautiful !"

And now, exciting no small stir amongst the tenants, grooms, stable-boys, and others who on various pretexts were crowding the entrance, the horses, urged on to speed by the postilion, dashed over the drawbridge, through the arched gateway into the paved courtyard, and stood chafed and foaming before the door, where the Hopes stood ready to receive the young master. Ernest had no time to gaze round on the romantic pile of building which surrounded him—the tower, the mullioned windows, the walls of massive stone, almost covered with various kinds of creepers; he was so anxious to have a sight of his new relations, who appeared at the entrance to welcome them. There was a rather stout gentleman, whom, from a family likeness to Charles, Ernest at once set down for his uncle; a tall, good-looking lady, in a superb silk dress that looked rich enough to stand upright by itself, and whose very rustle seemed to speak of formidable dignity; and a fairy-like young creature, a little older than himself, whom, at the first glance, Ernest thought exceedingly pretty.

Charles, accustomed from infancy to be a person of importance, sprang eagerly out of the carriage first, almost before the horses had stopped. He ran to his aunt. "Where is Lord Fontonore?" said she, passing him, and advancing to the door of the carriage. "Dear Clemmy!" exclaimed Charles, taking his cousin's hand, "how long it is since we have met!" She returned his press indeed, but her eyes were not looking towards him; she had not even a glance to give her old companion, so eagerly was her gaze turned in another direction.

"Is this the reception that I meet with?" thought Charles, anger and disappointment boiling in his heart. "It was then the peer whom they flattered and caressed; I am now only Charles Hope, and I must be deserted for the first stranger who has a title;" and without attending to the greeting of his uncle, or to that of the

servants, with whom he had always been a favourite,
Charles hurried off impatiently to his own room.

A beautiful room it was, all hung round with pictures.
There was one which Charles especially valued, the
portrait of his mother when she was a girl, with deep,

CHARLES AND HIS MOTHER'S PORTRAIT

thoughtful eyes, so much like Ernest's that Charles wondered that he had not recognized the resemblance the
first moment that he had seen his brother. This picture
had often exercised a soothing effect over the boy ; the
thought of his gentle mother now in heaven drew his

own affections thither; the hope of meeting her there was so sweet, the desire of being worthy of her so strong—for his mind had invested her with all the qualities of an angel—and the parent who had died before he could know his loss, was the object of the deepest tenderness of the boy.

"She, at least, is not changed—she looks always the same!" exclaimed Charles, clasping his hands, and gazing upon the portrait till his eyes became dimmed with tears. He was disturbed by a low knock at the door.

"Come in!" exclaimed Charles in an impatient tone, hastily dashing the moisture from his eyes. It was the housekeeper who appeared at the door.

"Please, my lord, Master Charles, I am sorry to disturb you, but this room Mrs. Hope desired to be prepared for Lord Fontonore; the blue room has been made ready for you."

Charles rushed out of the apartment without saying a word, in a passion of anger and resentment. The trial which he had seen but from a distance was now most keenly and bitterly felt. He locked his door, and paced backwards and forwards across the room, wishing that he could shut out all sound of voices and tread of feet, as he traced by it the progress of the party through the castle, which his relations were now showing to its new possessor. And thus he remained in his solitary misery, while Ernest painfully missed from his side one who was more to his affectionate heart than all the wealth of the world, and with an uncomfortable consciousness of his every motion being watched by those who regarded him rather with curiosity than interest, passed through long corridors, and stately apartments, which were expected to strike him with wonder.

"He is not so vulgar or funny as I expected that he would be," whispered Clementina to some one beside her; "but it makes me laugh to see him look so shy and uneasy, as if he were half afraid to look at his own castle. He certainly has a very interesting air, but he is not half so handsome as Charles."

CHAPTER XIV.

" WISH to see no one!" exclaimed Charles, as again a knock was heard at his door.

" Will you not admit me?" said the voice of Mr. Ewart. In an instant the door was thrown open.

"I did not know that it was you, sir; but I might have guessed who was the only being likely to come near me."

Mr. Ewart saw in a moment by the face of his pupil, as well as by the tone in which he spoke, that he was struggling—no, not struggling with, but rather overcome by his passions; and more grieved than displeased by the conduct of the boy, he led him quietly to a sofa, on which they both sat down together.

" I am sorry," said Mr. Ewart, " that you left us so soon ; your brother may be hurt by your absence."

" Oh, he'll never miss me ; he has plenty to take up his attention. Aunt Matilda will never let him out of her sight. Miss Clemmy will deck herself out even finer than usual to do honour to the lord of the castle. And of course he'll be taken by all the flattery and fuss; he'll believe all the nonsense of that worldly set; he'll be everything now, and I shall be nothing, because he happened to be born a year before me. It's very hard," he added bitterly; "it's very hard."

" ' *It's very hard* ' is one of the Evil One's favourite suggestions," said Mr. Ewart; "its meaning was contained in the very first words which he ever uttered to a human ear. He would have persuaded Eve that it was *very hard* that she might not eat of every fruit in the garden; and now, surrounded as we are with manifold blessings, it is his delight to point to the one thing denied, and still whisper, ' *It's very hard* to be kept from that which you so much desire.' "

" I cannot help feeling," murmured Charles; " things are so different now from what they were."

" Did you ever expect them to remain the same ? Did you suppose that your path would be always amongst flowers ? Are you not forgetting that you are a stranger and a pilgrim—the follower of a Master who was a man of sorrows ? "

Charles sighed heavily, and looked down.

" How often have you repeated the lines—

' The greatest evil we can fear,
Is to possess our portion here ! '

Had you the power of choice, would you enjoy that

portion in this life, were it even to bestow on you the crown of an emperor?"

"No," replied Charles, with emphasis.

"Let me refer you to your favourite Pilgrim's Progress. Remember what Christian beheld in the house of the Interpreter—that which we constantly behold in daily life: Passion demanding his treasure at once; Patience waiting meekly for a treasure to come. Which was the richest in the end?"

"You must not imagine that it was the sight of the dear old castle, and all that I have lost, that has made me feel in this way," exclaimed Charles. "You saw how cheerful I was not an hour ago, and I knew then that I was no longer Lord Fontonore."

"Yes; you had seen your cross, but you had not taken it up; you had not felt its weight. It is now that you must rouse up your courage."

"What I feel," exclaimed Charles impetuously, "is contempt for the mean, heartless beings, who were all kindness to me when I bore a title, and now have turned round like weathercocks! I do not believe that even you can defend them."

"I think that you may judge them hardly. You have too easily taken offence; you have made no allowance for their natural curiosity to see the hero of so romantic a tale as Ernest's. Would not you yourself have felt eager to meet him?"

Charles admitted that perhaps he might have done so.

"You have taken Passion and Pride for your counsellors, dear Charles : the one has blinded your eyes that
you should not see the straight path ; the other would
bind your feet that you should not pursue it. And
miserable counsellors have you found them both ; they
have inflicted on your heart more pain than the loss of
both title and estate."

"What would you have me do ?" said Charles, more
quietly ; for he felt the truth of the last observation.

"*First*, I would have you endeavour to bring yourself
to *be content to be of little importance.* Until your
mind is in this state of submission, you will be like one
with a wound which is being perpetually rubbed.

"*Secondly*, I would have you seek your earthly enjoyment rather in beholding that of others, than in any
pleasure that comes direct to yourself. Thus, in one
way, Fontonore will be yours still.

"*Thirdly*, I would have you prayerfully on the watch
against the slightest feeling of jealousy towards Ernest.
Never let your only brother think for one moment that
you feel that he stands in your way."

"Oh, Mr. Ewart !" cried Charles, starting to his feet,
"how could you imagine such a thing ?"

"It rests with you alone to prevent *his* thinking it,
and you have made a bad beginning to-day."

"I will go to Ernest at once," said the boy, "and

help to show him over the place. He shall never say—
he shall never think that I am envious of his prosperity."

In truth, on that first evening of his arrival in the
castle, Ernest was not much to be envied. He was
uneasy about his brother—uncomfortable with his new
companions ; one hearty grasp from the hand of Charles,
or approving word from his tutor, was worth all the
smiles, and courtesies, and bows, which he knew had
nothing to do with the heart. Ernest felt himself out
of his natural place, and was constantly afraid of saying
or doing something that would shock the polished gran-
dees around him. As far as speaking was concerned, he
was indeed tolerably safe, for he scarcely opened his lips,
which made his companions set him down as dull and
stupid ; but he had been accustomed for so short a time
to the refinements of polished society, and was so likely,
in his very anxiety to please, to forget even the hints
that he had received from Mr. Ewart, that there was
certainly some little danger of his doing something
"shocking." The presence of half-a-dozen footmen in
gay liveries in the room, was a disagreeable piece of
state to the young lord ; so many eyes were turned upon
him whenever he moved ; there were so many listeners if
he uttered a word !

Ernest made the serious mistake of eating fish with
a knife. The shocked look of his aunt made him
sensible of his blunder, and covered his face with blushes.

At another time, Clementina pressed her lace handkerchief over her lips, to stifle her too evident inclination to
titter, at the peasant-bred peer helping her to something
from the dish before him with his own spoon. Ernest
was very glad when the dinner was over, which had
lasted, indeed, nearly twice as long as any of which he
had ever partaken before.

After dinner, Clementina was desired by her mother to
go to the piano and play. She made so many excuses,
said that she was tired, nervous, out of practice, that
Ernest, little practised in the ways of Vanity Fair, was
inclined to beg that the young lady might be let off.
Great would have been her mortification had he done so,
however—the girl was only refusing in order to be
pressed; the virtue of sincerity, if she had ever possessed
it, had all been frittered away by folly. She sat down
to the instrument, determined to be admired; for admiration to her was as the very breath of life. She played
what might be called a very brilliant piece—full of
shakes, dashes, and runs, but with no melody at all.
Ernest, though fond of music, thought it certainly not
pretty, and, had he been more at his ease, could hardly
have helped laughing at the affected air of the young
performer, and the manner in which she threw up her
hands, and sometimes her eyes also, in the slower movements of the piece. Every motion appeared to be
studied : self was never for a moment forgotten. When

CLEMENTINA AT THE PIANO.

the performance, rather to Ernest's relief, was concluded, with a satisfied look the stately mother turned to the young peer, and asked him if that was not a beautiful piece. "Rather," replied Ernest, after a little hesita-

tion, as much vexed with himself for saying so much
as Clementina was at his saying so little.   Charles, who
was standing near, could not avoid laughing ; and Ernest
read in the eyes of Mrs. Hope her unexpressed thought
—" I have no patience for this low, ill-bred boor !"

With a secret feeling of constraint, mortification, and
disappointment, poor Ernest retired at night to his own
room.   Two maids were preparing it as he entered, and
he could not help overhearing the words of one of them,—

" 'Tis a pity that Master Charles was not the eldest son."

" I'm sure that I think so !" Ernest exclaimed, aloud,
to the no small surprise of the girl who had uttered the
observation.

CHAPTER XV.

HERE was another matter that weighed upon the mind of Ernest, and was his first thought when he awoke in the morning. It was the request which he was to make to his uncle concerning bringing Jack and Ben to the castle. Mr. Ewart had declined making the request for him, and in this Ernest thought his tutor for the first time unkind. But Ernest was mistaken, as those usually are who judge others without entering into their feelings or position. The truth was that Mr. Ewart very well knew that no request made by him would be likely to be granted. He was almost disliked by Mr. Hope, whose character presented a remarkable contrast to his own, and who treated his nephews' tutor with bare civility, though as well born and better educated than himself.

Mr. Hope was what is called a man of the world— one who made business his sole ambition; his worldliness, his pride, were in the sight of the Eternal but— vanity !

Ernest was beginning to more than waver in his wish to have the sons of Lawless living so near him. He felt since his arrival at Fontonore, more than he had ever done before, how disagreeable their presence might be. Had Ernest not been a sincere Christian, he would have tried as much as possible to banish from his mind all recollection of early days of humiliation and suffering, and would have endeavoured to keep far away from himself all that could remind him of his peasant life. But Ernest felt that this would be throwing away the lessons which God had taught him at the cost of so much pain ; and that, in failing to bring those whom he had once considered his brothers to a place where they might benefit from the same instructions that had been so much blessed to himself, he might be neglecting the means of bringing them to God.

Ernest therefore resolved to speak to his uncle, much as he disliked doing so ; and he found an opportunity the very first morning, as Mr. Hope sat alone in the library engaged in reading the *Times*.

"Did you want a book, Ernest?" said his uncle, as the young nobleman stood hesitating and embarrassed before him. "You'll have to make up for lost time, I suspect. Let's see, how old are you now?"

"I was twelve last March," replied Ernest.

"Ah, I remember—in your thirteenth year; you should have made some progress by that age. I suppose that your studies have been much neglected. May I ask what books you have read?"

"The Bible and Pilgrim's Progress," answered the boy.

Mr. Hope turned down the corners of his mouth with a contemptuous expression, little dreaming that all the treasures of learning and wit which the most talented mind ever grasped are useless—worthless, compared with the wisdom to be gathered from one sacred volume.

"A puritanical library, more select than comprehensive," said the gentleman; "you must apply yourself to something else in future. You have a pretty long course of education before you ere you can be fit for the station which you hold—Latin, Greek, French, German, mathematics, algebra, natural philosophy, and a thousand other things, indispensable for a nobleman—all to be mastered in the next few years."

Ernest felt himself at the foot of a new mountain of difficulty, with a humiliating sense of ignorance.

"But you wished to say something to me," resumed Mr. Hope, leaning back in his chair, and laying down the paper with a formidable air of attention.

"Now for it!" thought Ernest, struggling against his shyness and his extreme disinclination to speak to his uncle. "Sir," said he aloud, "I am very anxious to do something for my bro— the sons of Lawless, I mean, with whom I passed the days of my childhood."

"If I might advise, you would never allude to those days."

Ernest coloured, yet encouraged himself by remembering that there is nothing but guilt which need cause us shame, and that we should blush for no situation in which Heaven has placed us. "I would wish, if you consent, to bring the boys here," resumed he, "and place them under care of the gardener."

"An extraordinary wish," replied Mr. Hope, taking snuff. "Is it possible that this is really your desire?"

"I am most anxious for your leave to do it," said Ernest.

"Oh, of course, if you have no objection, I can have none; this is your own property, and it is only reasonable that you should have a voice in choosing your dependants. But all that I can say is, that I believe that you'll repent it, and the young rogues would be better in the poor-house."

Ernest left his uncle's presence rather in spirits, from having accomplished his object more easily than he had expected. He cheerfully pursued his studies with Charles, under the tuition of Mr. Ewart; and the consideration which they showed—never laughing at his mistakes, ever ready to help him to understand what was new to him—still further endeared them both to the boy.

After luncheon, feeling a little more at his ease, as

Mrs. Hope sat busy at her writing-desk, and her husband was not in the room, Ernest amused himself with his pretty little cousin, Clementina, in looking over a large volume of prints.

"What a pity that she is so affected!" thought he; "she would be so charming if she did not think herself so."

On a sudden Ernest jumped up with an exclamation of pleasure, as he saw from the window a little open carriage approaching through the park.

"Oh, I'm so glad!—there are good, kind Mr. and Miss Searle; it will be such a pleasure to see them!"

"The old horrors!" exclaimed Clementina, leaning back on her cushions, and lifting her hands in affected alarm.

"The Searles!" cried Mrs. Hope, looking up hastily. "We're not at home to them. I'm surprised at their coming. People like them never know their proper place. I must request, Ernest," she continued, seeing him about to leave the room, "that you'll not bring such company about the castle. When you are of age, of course, you'll do what you please; but while I and my daughter remain under this roof, I must be careful not to expose her to vulgar society. Mr. Searle's father kept a shop in Cheapside!"

"Vulgar!" thought Ernest, "some of the excellent of the earth! The Lord's jewels, at whose feet we may one day be thankful to be found! Is this castle too grand, its inhabitants too good, for those whose home will be heaven, whose companions the angels?"

Mrs. Hope, as the reader may have observed, was a very proud woman, one ready to worship rank, whoever might possess it. She was of rather low origin herself, which was perhaps one reason why she always avowed herself most particular in regard to the company that she kept. No virtue, with her, could weigh against a coronet; she valued her acquaintance—for such characters have few *friends*—according to their position in society. To be a companion of the nobility was her delight; to become one of them was the object of her highest ambition. For this she encouraged her husband's efforts for advancement, and had been delighted to see him a Member for Parliament. Her own poor relations were, of course, kept at a distance; no one bearing her maiden name of Briggs had ever been known to cross the threshold of Castle Fontonore except her brother, an attorney, who once ventured in, but was never even asked to break bread in the house, and who left his sister's presence with a clouded brow, and a determination never to trouble her again. The proud worldly woman never reflected that in another state, where the high and the low, the great and the humble, shall meet together, her love of distinction, her pride of display, should appear as lighter than vanity.

What could be expected from the daughter of such a parent? Even a strong mind might have been ruined by the education which she received; and Clementina, who was naturally of but slender intellect, was quite spoiled by the society in which she was brought up. At a fashionable school she had learned a few accomplishments, and a great deal of folly : admiration, amusement, excitement, these were the three things upon which her whole heart was set; all that she lived for was comprised in these three words. The quiet serenity of a soul that rests on one unchanging object, was of course never known to her. The slightest incident was sufficient to raise her spirits to a wild height, or sink them to the point of misery; she was transported at an invitation to a ball, wretched if a dressmaker failed her. She was like a fluttering butterfly, shining in its gay colours, driven about by every breeze on its unsteady, uncertain course. But I wrong the insect in making the comparison. The butterfly fills its allotted place in creation—it does all that its Maker intended it to do; while the frivolous, silly, selfish girl remains a blank, or rather a blot, in God's world, when she who is called to the work and the destiny of angels makes that of a butterfly her deliberate choice.

It is just possible that some thoughtless girl, whose education and character may resemble Clementina's, may in some vacant hour of leisure turn over the leaves of my little book. Oh, that I had an angel's voice, to rouse her to a sense of what she is and what she might be! to make her feel that she is not her own, but *bought with a price*, such a price as the world could not have paid ;—that a soul which must exist for ever and ever—that a soul for which a God bled, agonized, and died—is a thing too noble, a thing too precious to be thrown away at Vanity Fair.

CHAPTER XVI.

THE Sabbath came, God's holy day, and the family attended a church which was at some little distance. Mr. and Mrs. Hope and their daughter, the ladies arrayed in all the splendour of fashion, went in state in the carriage, with two footmen in attendance, while the boys preferred walking over the fields with their tutor.

Ernest, as he entered the church, drew the eyes of the whole congregation upon himself, which made him more uncomfortable than ever. " Am I not to escape even here from Vanity Fair?" thought he; "cannot even these walls shut out the world ! "

Straight in front of the seat which he occupied was a marble monument of singular beauty, which naturally attracted his attention. It represented the figure of a very lovely babe, sleeping amongst water-lilies, the attitude and countenance depicting the peaceful slumber of innocence. Below was an inscription, which the boy read with strange emotion :—

IN MEMORY OF

ERNEST,

ELDEST SON OF THE FIRST LORD FONTONORE.

WHO WAS ACCIDENTALLY DROWNED

BEFORE HE HAD COMPLETED THE

FIRST YEAR OF HIS AGE.

" 'Tis thus the snow-flake from the skies,
    Touching the sod, dissolves and dies ;
    Ere mists of earth can its whiteness stain,
    Raised by the sunbeams to heaven again.

" Though parted now on life's thorny way,
    'Twere weak, 'twere cruel, to wish his stay ;
    We must toil on through trials, griefs, alarms —
    He was borne to the goal in his Saviour's arms."

After service was over, Clementina took a fancy—for
she was always governed by fancies—to walk home
with her cousins instead of driving with her parents.
She therefore pursued the path across the fields with
Ernest, whilst Charles and his tutor walked a little way
behind.

"I was so much diverted at church," said the young
lady, in the flippant manner which she mistook for wit,
" I was so much diverted to see you looking so seriously
at the inscription upon your own monument. It was
so funny, I could hardly help bursting out laughing,
only that would have been very improper, you know."

"The inscription made me feel anything but inclined
to laugh," observed Ernest.

"Well, I would give the world,"—had the world belonged to Clementina, she would have given it away ten times a-day,—"I would give the world to know what you were thinking when you read those fine verses upon yourself."

"I was thinking whether it would indeed have been happier for me to have died when I was a little one, before I had known anything of the world and sin."

"Oh, dear me! those are the dreadful, gloomy notions which you get from your horrid, methodistical tutor."

"Clementina, I will not hear him spoken of in that manner," said Ernest, with a decision of tone which the young lady had never heard him make use of before. She was either offended, or thought it pretty to look so, for stopping as they reached a very low stile, she called to Charles to help her over it. She wished to vex Ernest, and raise a feeling of jealousy toward his brother; but she was successful in neither of her designs, as Ernest very contentedly turned back to Mr. Ewart, and left the fair lady to pursue her walk with the companion whom she had chosen.

"I am so sorry for you, dear Charles!" said Clementina, in a voice rather more affected than usual; "it is so dreadful to be turned out of your right by a low, vulgar creature like that."

"But you see I don't think him either low or vulgar," replied Charles, good humouredly. "He has high

RETURNING FROM CHURCH.

feelings, and high principles; and as for being vulgar, a boy who thinks so much, and upon such subjects as he does, can never, as Mr. Ewart said to me once, have a vulgar mind."

"I find him intolerably dull," said Clementina.

" I am sorry for it," was her cousin's dry reply.

Clementina was now offended with Charles in his turn, and had there been a third party less unmanageable than Mr. Ewart, she would doubtless have chosen him to accompany her, in the delightful hope of annoying both her cousins. The silly girl was almost unconsciously forming a plan to separate the brothers, and

make them jealous of each other, by sometimes favour-
ing the elder, sometimes the younger, so as to draw their
whole attention towards herself. You may think that it
was some unkind and bitter feeling that made her wish
thus to destroy their happiness and union, and act the part
of a tempter towards her companions; but it was nothing
but selfish vanity and folly—so that she was amused, she
cared not who suffered ; the power to give pain she considered as a triumph—it is reckoned so in Vanity Fair.

She turned round to see if Ernest were watching her
movements, but was extremely provoked to find him so
deeply engaged in serious conversation with the clergyman, that her presence seemed altogether forgotten.
Clementina had therefore no resource but to walk on
with Charles, doing her best to put all the sermon out
of his head, by rattling on about her delight at the prospect of soon going to London, her distress at its not
being the gay season, her conviction that young ladies
ought to come out at fourteen, how she was charmed at
the prospect held out of a child's ball in Grosvenor
Square, but in despair at the dear countess not being in
town ! Such is the conversation of Vanity Fair.

In the afternoon Mrs. Hope informed Ernest of the
intended move, which circumstances had led her to
make earlier than she had intended. " I propose remaining in London till after Christmas," she said; " of
course you and your brother will accompany us."

" And Mr. Ewart ?"

" There is no room in our town house for him,"
replied the lady, who, like her husband, had little love
for one, the unworldliness of whose character seemed a
silent reproach upon her own.

" It would surely be a great pity that I should leave
my studies," said Ernest; "pray remember how much
time I have lost already."

" Oh, I've quite decided on your coming. To acquire
a fashionable air, and the good breeding of the *haut-ton*,
is quite as indispensable as any book-learning."

The truth was that the lady had no idea of losing an
opportunity of displaying to her acquaintance her
nephew, the young peer.

On the following evening Charles came to his brother,
who was engaged in the dry study of a Latin grammar,
to announce to him the arrival of Jack and Ben, who
had just been landed at the gardener's cottage.

" I must go and see them at once," said Ernest,
rising.

" 'Tis late and cold ; I think that you might wait
till to-morrow."

" Oh no ; they are strangers here, poor boys, they
have none but me to bid them welcome."

" Then I'll go with you to see the meeting," said
Charles, taking down his cap from its peg.

There was something of awkwardness, a little mixed

with fear, in the manner of Ben, as the young nobleman kindly held out his hand to him ; but Jack had
lost none of his own reckless, impudent air, and strangely
did his voice remind Ernest of former days as he called
out, as if still in his cottage on the common, " I say,
Mark, here's a fine change for you !"

" I don't believe that the boy knows how to blush,"
whispered Charles.

" But I hope that you don't mean to keep us long
here," continued Jack, looking round rather contemp-
tuously on the clean little dwelling.

" What do you mean ? " replied Ernest ; " surely you
prefer it to the poor-house ! "

" Why, you don't think that I'll stand living in a
cottage, while my brother is in a castle ! That would
be rather a good joke I should say."

" He's no brother of yours," cried Charles, angrily.

" I'm as good as he any day," muttered the boy,
glancing at Ernest with mingled envy and dislike. The
young peer mastered his temper, though it cost him an
effort. " I have placed you," said he, " where one much
wiser than either of us thinks that you will be best ; I
hope that you will be comfortable, and learn your work,
and never have real cause to regret coming here." With
these words Ernest and Charles quitted the cottage,
overhearing as they passed out Ben's disappointed exclamation, " I thought he'd have made us gentlefolk too!"

"How hard it is to do good!" said Ernest, with a sigh of mortification, when they had walked a few steps from the place. "I see the wisdom of Mr. Ewart's doubts, when he said that he believed that there might be objections to this plan."

"Well, you've acted kindly, and you'll have your reward," observed Charles.

"Not in the gratitude of these boys."

"Did you do it to purchase their gratitude?" asked his brother. "Mr. Ewart says that some do good actions to buy praise, and some to buy gratitude, but both look for an earthly reward, and, therefore, for one which can never be sure. It is the cup of cold water given for the Lord's sake which is remembered and rewarded above."

"True," replied Ernest, "and if we do good only in order to be loved, the many, many disappointments which we meet with, will soon make us weary in well-doing. That benevolence only will be steady and sure which comes from a wish to please that Master in heaven who never can change or forget."

CHAPTER XVII

AYS and weeks passed, but the instructions which he received seemed to make little impression on the obdurate spirit of Jack, who had one idea rooted in his mind, which neither example nor exhortation was able to shake— that it was a sort of injustice to him for one who had once been his equal to be so rich while he remained so poor. In vain both the folly and ingratitude of his conduct were shown to him; a proud, levelling spirit had taken possession of his heart, which would neither bend in submission to Heaven, nor thankfulness to those who did him kindness. Would that this feeling were more uncommon in the dwellings of the humbler classes, and that they to whom little of this world's goods have been given would remember that, while the rich have duties towards the poor, the poor have also duties towards the rich.

The annoyance which it caused Ernest's sensitive spirit to be the object of envy and ingratitude, and the necessity of being ever on his guard to avoid expressing anger, or, which is much harder, feeling it, made him rather rejoice when the day arrived for the family's removal to London. He was impatient to see that wonderful place of which he had heard so much. The winter, also, had come, and the coldness of the weather made the prospect of a journey southwards very agreeable. The boy's only regret was leaving Mr. Ewart, whom they regarded more as a parent than a tutor.

"Good-bye, and Heaven watch over you!" said the clergyman, earnestly, as he stood at the door to witness their departure.

Charles pressed his tutor's hand warmly between both his own ; Ernest threw himself into his arms.

"You must not keep us, boys ; we shall be late for the train," called out Mr. Hope from the carriage.

"I can't conceive what makes them so fond of that man," observed Mrs. Hope in no amiable tone.

"You will see more of Vanity Fair," said the clergyman, in a low voice ; "I have but one word for you,— *Watch and pray, lest ye enter into temptation!*"

The next moment the carriage dashed across the court-yard ; Mr. Ewart followed it through the arched gateway, and stood on the drawbridge which crossed the moat, watching till he could no longer see his dear pupils standing up in the carriage and waving to him.

A railway journey was a new thing to Ernest, and

raised many thoughts in his mind as the train rushed rattling along the line, sometimes raised on a causeway, sometimes sunk in a cutting, sometimes lost in the dark-

THE PARTING WITH MR. EWART.

ness of a tunnel; yet, whether above the surrounding country or below it, whether in brightness or whether in gloom, rushing on—on—on, with wondrous speed, towards the goal to which each hour brought it nearer.

"I, too, have had my dark portions of the journey, and now Heaven has been pleased to raise me," thought Ernest, "and the sunshine is bright around me. But when I arrive at the end of my journey, how little I shall care whether it was long or short, through gloom or light, uncomfortable or pleasant, it will be enough if it has taken me to my *home!*"

And now let us see our young pilgrims settled in London—in that wonderful assemblage of all that is noblest and all that is basest in the world; the abode of the greatest wealth and the most abject poverty; the seat of learning, arts, science, crime, misery, and ignorance; the city which contains at once perhaps more good and more evil than any other spot on the face of the globe. Ernest found his expectations more than realized as regards its size; there seemed no end to the wilderness of brick houses—street crossing street to form a mighty labyrinth which both astonishes and confuses the mind. The unceasing roll of carriages and stream of passers-by; the variety of vehicles of all kinds and shapes; the innumerable shops; the stately public buildings, churches, hospitals, schools, and places of amusement—all had the charm of novelty to the young noble, and fresh impressions were made upon his mind every hour.

Then came a round of all the diversions which London could offer at that period of the year. Days and nights, also, were crowded with amusements; and Ernest, at first in a whirl of pleasure, soon began to experience the weariness of a life devoted to gaiety. His mind felt clogged with the multitude of new ideas; his head ached from confinement in crowded rooms; his rest was broken in upon; he became almost knocked up by excitement, more tired than he had ever before been made by labour, without the satisfaction of gaining anything by his fatigue. He began to long for the quiet of Fontonore again, and to exchange the bustle of gaiety into which he was plunged, for calm study and the society of Mr. Ewart.

And how fared the spiritual health of the pilgrim?— was he making progress towards heaven, or falling back? Ernest had entered London forewarned and forearmed; circumstances, not choice, were leading him through the very midst of Vanity Fair, but he was walking as a pilgrim still. He had made a prayerful resolution from the very beginning, to devote the first hour of each morning to God. Sloth, increased by weariness, often tempted him to break this resolution on the cold wintry mornings, and suggested many an excuse for self-in-dulgence. But Ernest knew that he stood upon dangerous ground, and kept resolute to his purpose; and that quiet hour for communion with his own heart, for self-examination, reading of the Scripture, and prayer, was his great safeguard amidst the numerous temptations which encompassed him in his new path of life. Things which, only seen in the torch-glare of worldly excitement, must always have appeared in false colours, reviewed in the pure light of morning lost much of their dangerous attractions. I cannot too earnestly recommend to all, whether young or old, in high or low estate, thus to give their first hours to God.

The family assembled so late for breakfast, that Ernest found that, by a little self-denial, he might not only have time for devotion, but also for study in the morning. He was exceedingly anxious to cultivate his mind; he felt his deficiencies very painful, and he was sometimes even tempted to encroach on his "holy hour," as he called it, to have more time for improving his intellect. This is a temptation which probably some of my readers have known, and which is all the more dangerous because it does not shock the conscience so much as other ways of passing the time. But still Ernest kept as free as he could from any earthly occupation the precious little space where, apart from the world, he could collect his strength and renew his good resolutions.

The only member of the family who gave him the least assistance in treading the heavenward way was his brother; and often did Ernest think of the wisdom and mercy of the Saviour in sending His disciples by two and two into the world. The characters of the boys were in some points very unlike, but there was one hope, one guiding principle, in both, and perhaps the very difference in their dispositions made them more able to support one another. Ernest was more shy and diffident than his brother, but had a deeper knowledge of his own heart. Charles had learned more, but Ernest had reflected more; Charles was in more danger from love of the world, Ernest from shrinking too much from its ridicule. Where Hope was impatient, Fontonore had learned to wait: their early life had been passed in different schools—one the child of luxury, the other of want; one tried by pleasure, the other by suffering; but both had passed through the strait wicket-gate; both were united in sincere love to the Saviour; both were anxious to struggle against their besetting sins, and to press onward to the prize set before them.

Would that we were ever as ready to help one another in the narrow path as these two young Christian pilgrims! If, instead of acting, as we too often do, the part either of tempters or tormentors, we employed all the influence which friendship and relationship give us to draw our companions nearer to heaven, what a blessing would rest on our intercourse below! How much would it resemble that which we hope to enjoy above!

One thing which the inexperienced Ernest soon discovered was, that money disappeared very rapidly in London. That which at first had seemed to him an inexhaustible fortune, appeared almost as though it melted away in his hand. One of his first cares on entering the capital was to procure a most beautiful Bible, and send it, with a grateful letter, to Miss Searle. This was at once a pleasure and a relief to his heart, for it had been burdened—not with a sense of owing kindness, for that is painful only to the proud spirit, but the feeling that he might appear ungrateful, and that those who had been his friends in adversity might think that in his prosperity he had forgotten them.

Then there were so many necessary things to be purchased—so many tempting books to be desired, for Ernest delighted in reading—so many charities which he wished to aid—so many objects of pity that he yearned to relieve, that the youthful nobleman's once heavy purse soon became very empty.

Ernest had been some time in London before he went to visit Madge, in the asylum in which he was supporting her. He reproached himself with the delay; but, in truth, the conduct of her brothers had so disheartened him, that it was as a duty, and no pleasure, that he went there at all. Charles, as usual, was his companion, and his only one; for visiting charities was little in the way either of his uncle or his proud wife, though Mrs. Hope had once held a stall at a grand Fancy fair, which was patronized by duchesses and countesses. As for Clementina, she would never have dreamed of going; she had a vague connection in her mind between poverty and dirt, and thought it dreadful if a child of the lower classes ventured to approach within two yards of her. Many a tear had the young lady shed over a novel : for heroes and heroines she had ready sympathy ; she considered that sentiment and feeling give an added charm to beauty ; but common every-day sufferings had in them nothing " interesting." She could be touched by the sorrow of a princess, but the real wants of a ragged child were quite beneath her regard.

Ernest was agreeably surprised in the asylum. Everything so neat, so perfectly clean ; such an appearance of respectability in the matron, of health and good discipline amongst the children. Poor little Madge, also, was so much delighted to see a face that she knew, after being only surrounded by strangers, that Ernest felt vexed with himself for not visiting her sooner, and emptied his purse of its last half-crown to place in the hand of the child. This still further opened the heart of Madge, and she talked to him almost as freely as if she had still regarded him as her brother, though without the insolent familiarity which was so repulsive in Jack.

She showed Ernest a letter which she had received from her unhappy mother, who had been sentenced to transportation, though for a shorter period than her husband, on account of being specially recommended to mercy. Ernest had, through Mr. Ewart, provided Ann with some little comforts ; and to this, in her letter, she gratefully alluded, though his kindness, she wrote, only made her feel more wrétched, when she remembered how cruelly she had wronged him. She implored her daughter to shun the temptations which had led her astray, especially the love of dress, the beginning of all her errors and her misery—the vanity which had laid her open to flattery, and had made her take the first step in that downward course which had led her to prison and a convict-ship. There was deep remorse expressed in the letter, which gave Ernest hopes that the poor prodigal might yet repent and find mercy; but its tone of cheerless gloom showed but too well that the mire of the Slough of Despond was clinging to the unhappy one still.

Perfectly satisfied with Mr. Ewart's choice of a home for the more than orphan girl, Ernest quitted the asylum with his brother, thankful that an opportunity had been granted him of repaying evil with good. He was enabled to provide for three children, whose parents had inflicted on him deep injuries, and from whom he had received, during the years of childhood, unkindness which had imbittered his life. It is easier to forgive one great wrong than a long course of petty provocations; and when both are united to rouse the spirit of revenge, nothing but grace given to us from Heaven can make us forgive as we have been forgiven.

As the brothers passed a bookseller's shop, on their way home, Charles paused to look at a volume in the window.

"Oh, Ernest," he exclaimed, "look what a beautiful copy is there of that work which Mr. Ewart so much wished to see! Do let us buy it for him, as a New-Year's gift, to take back with us to Fontonore. My funds are rather low; but if we join purses, we shall easily make out the sum together."

"I really cannot," replied Ernest, looking wistfully at the beautiful book.

"Oh, but you must! You know," said Charles, lowering his voice to a whisper, "that Mr. Ewart never procures these indulgences for himself. I believe, from what I heard my uncle say, that he entirely supports an aged mother. I never knew him spend an unnecessary shilling on himself."

"Perhaps the book is in our library," suggested Ernest.

"It is not; it was his hunting all over it for the work that made me know how much he wished to have it. I wonder, Ernest," added Charles, with a little temper, "that one rolling in wealth like you should make such a fuss about a few shillings."

"I am not rolling in wealth at present," answered Ernest, rather vexed at his brother's tone; "I have not a shilling left in my purse."

"Then you must have been wondrously extravagant. Why, even I, on my half-allowance, have managed to keep a little silver, and I was never famous for economy."

Ernest made no reply.

"We had better go on," said Charles.

They walked on for some time in silence.

"I am afraid that I spoke rudely to you just now; will you forgive me?" said Hope, at last.

"Oh, do not talk about forgiveness," replied Ernest, cheerfully. "I think that I could forgive you anything; and one should never take offence at a word."

"I ought to have remembered," observed Charles, "that the child whom we have just seen is a great expense to you; and yet you seem to spend so little, that I hardly fancied that you could have got through the allowance of a whole quarter. Do you not receive the same sum that I used to have when I imagined myself to be Lord Fontonore?"

"No," replied his brother, and immediately changed the conversation.

They walked on for some distance, talking on other matters, when, as they were passing through one of the parks, Charles stopped, as if some thought had suddenly crossed his mind.

"Ernest," said he, laying his hand on his brother's arm, "just answer me one question : How is it that you do not receive the same allowance that I did?" Receiving no answer, he continued, "Is it possible that you are dividing yours with me?"

Ernest smiled. "I am not bound to answer questions," said he.

THE CONVERSATION IN THE PARK.

"Oh, I see it all! generous, noble-hearted brother! And you suffered me to accuse you in my own mind of meanness—almost to reproach you to your face for it—while all the time it was your money that I have been spending, and you never even let me know my obligation!"

"Obligation is not a word for brothers," replied Ernest; "what I have is yours; what you spend I enjoy; let us always have a common purse between us."

"No, that must never be!" exclaimed Charles; "you

have burdens enough upon your hands already. My uncle must supply me."

"Do not deprive your brother of his privilege," said Ernest, who had seen enough of Mr. Hope by this time to know that it would be galling to Charles to be in any way dependent upon him. "You will hurt me if you deny me this favour; I shall think that you do not care for me, Charley."

It was the first time that Ernest had ever used this familiar and endearing name to his brother. There was something in his tone, as he pronounced it, and in his manner, as he threw his arm round Charles, that raised a glow of affection in the heart of the boy, warmer than he had ever known before. Both felt the strength of that holy beautiful tie by which the members of every family should be united. Children of the same parents on earth, children of the same Father in heaven; with one common home both below and above—one path to tread and one goal to reach—how is it that pride and envy can ever disunite the hearts which God himself would join together?

CHAPTER XVIII.

NE evening, after the family had been more than a month in London, Ernest sat alone in the drawing-room with his book. Mr. and Mrs. Hope were absent at a dinner party, which the lady was to leave early, in order to call for the young people, to take them to the long-expected ball in Grosvenor Square.

Clementina had been up-stairs for more than an hour, engaged in what was to her one of the most interesting occupations of life—decking out her little person in all the extravagance of fashion. Ernest sat by the window, not that the light by which he read was in any way derived from anything outside it; but it amused him to glance up occasionally from his page and look out upon what was to him a novel sight—a regular yellow London fog.

Of the long line of lamps which stretched down the street, only the two or three nearest were visible at all, and they looked like dim stars surrounded by a haze.

Loud shouts, sometimes mixed with laughter, were occasionally heard from foot-passengers wishing to give notice of their presence. Now two lights, like a pair of eyes, would slowly approach, marking where a carriage moved on its dangerous way; then torches carried past would throw a strange red glare on the fog, scarcely sufficient to show who bore them.

"We see something like this in life," said Ernest to himself. "I think that fog is the common weather of Vanity Fair. Let me see in how many points I can find a resemblance between nature's mists and those raised by 'the world.' Both come not from heaven, but belong to things below; both shut out the pure light of day—make us in danger of falling—in danger of striking against others—hardly able to tell friend from foe. Yet people seem particularly merry in both, as if the very risk were a pleasure. They light those glaring torches, and walk cheerfully on, though they can see neither sun, moon, nor stars. Who would wish to pass all his life in a fog? Yet some choose to live and die amidst the mists of Vanity Fair."

"Reading, moralizing, reflecting," said Charles, in his own lively manner, as he entered the room. "Who would take you for a young nobleman going to a ball? It will be your last for a long time, I suspect; for Parliament, I hear, is dissolved, and if so, there will be a new election, and back we must fly to Fontonore."

"I am not sorry for it," replied Ernest.

"Nor I," said Charles, more gravely. "I am afraid that this is a dangerous sort of life for me. You never seem to be in the same peril as myself; I suppose because you are a better pilgrim."

"Oh no!" exclaimed Ernest; "you cannot look into my heart; but every one knows his own temptations best. The truth is, that I cannot enjoy society so much, because I always feel that I am not sufficiently educated, and am in constant fear of exposing myself, and being laughed at. There is no possible merit in this."

"No; if that is all your protection from worldliness, I should call it a very poor one."

"Yes; for if it protects me on the one side, it exposes me to danger on the other. Do you know, Charles, that nothing astonishes me so much in myself, as the cowardice that I find that I possess."

"You manage well, for no one finds it out but yourself."

"I must care for the world, or I should not fear its ridicule. I was always thought rather courageous before I became a peer; I know that I used to speak out truth pretty boldly in our cottage; but there is nothing that I dread so much as the quiet sarcastic smile on well-bred lips. I sometimes fancy," he added, laughing, "that I should mind it less if there were any chance of its being followed by a blow."

"Well, this much I can say for you, Ernest—1 have never yet seen this fear draw you one step from the narrow path."

"I could not say as much for myself, dear brother. The world is a dangerous place."

"Which would you call the principal temptations of Vanity Fair?" said Charles.

"Temptations to be insincere, ill-natured, and forgetful of God."

"Oh, you have not numbered half. Think of all the extravagance, vanity, love of show, love of fashion, love of dress, love of trifles of all sorts."

"Which do not make us happy," added Ernest.

"Happy! no. They remind me of the beautiful enchanted money in the Eastern tale, which a man put so carefully by, and which he found, a short time after, all turned into leaves. Have you seen Clemmy on this evening of the ball, which she has been looking forward to for so long with such pleasure?"

"No; is she in very high spirits?"

"She is quite miserable, poor girl. I daresay that she would cry heartily, did she not know that red eyes are not becoming."

"What is vexing her so much?"

"She has three terrible troubles, which she knows not how to bear. Firstly, she fears that Aunt Matilda may not find her way in the fog, so may never call to take

us to the ball ; secondly, she fears that even if we should
reach Grosvenor Square, we should find the rooms empty
on such a night as this, and there would be few to admire
her and her new dress ; and, thirdly, she is afraid that
her pearl ornaments will not come in time ; and this is
her worst misery of all."

"Have they not arrived yet?"

"No ; Clemmy has been in a fidget about them all
day, starting at the sound of every bell with a cry of,
'Oh, I hope that's the jeweller at last?'   And since she
went up to dress, Mrs. Clayton has been sent down three
times at least to see if the ornaments have come ; and
as she has had always to return with the same unsatis-
factory answer, Clemmy is doubtless by this time in a
state of grief which might make her an object of pity to
any beggar in the street."

"Poor Clemmy!" murmured Ernest, with real compassion in his tone.

"You do not pity her, surely, for being unhappy at
such trifles?"

"I pity her because such trifles can make her unhappy.   Charles, do you know that my conscience is
not quite easy about our cousin?"

"Your conscience!   You have nothing to do with her
folly."

"We have a good deal to do with one another.   I see
more of her than of any one but yourself; she is one of

my nearest relations; and yet I have never tried in any way to help her on in the right path."

"I do not believe that she is in it," replied Charles. "She is constantly trying to play us off against each other; nothing would delight her so much as to make us quarrel, all to gratify her selfish vanity."

"If she is not in the right path, in which must she be? Where will she find herself if she remains as she is?"

"We cannot help her wanderings; they are no fault of ours."

"Oh, Charles, we must not act in the spirit of those words, 'Am I my brother's keeper?' We who meet her so often *must* have some influence for evil or good; and think of the rapture of meeting in heaven with one whom we had been the means of helping to reach it!"

"I can hardly fancy any delight greater," said Charles; "but I do not know anything that we could do for Clemmy. It is foolish in me, but when I look at her, and watch her affected manner, and hear her trifling talk, I never can realize to myself that she has a soul at all."

"Yet she has one just as precious as our own."

"I know that, but I cannot feel it; she seems just like a pretty plaything, made to be dressed up, admired —or laughed at."

"Would that she could be raised to something nobler, something better!"

"I do not believe that we can raise her. She only thinks me provoking, and you tiresome. She never would listen to Mr. Ewart, and I do believe only goes to church to show off the fashions. I do not see what we could do for her."

"We can pray, dear Charles, we can pray earnestly; if we have not done so before, we have neglected a duty."

"My neglect has been greater than yours," said his brother, "since we have been together for so many years. I have thought it enough if I were not led to folly by her society; I never dreamed that I had any other responsibility about her."

"But now—"

"Now I feel that I have been wrong. I remember, Ernest, that Faithful roused some to become pilgrims even in Vanity Fair; Hopeful himself was one of them. Perhaps poor Clemmy—"

"Here she comes; I hear the rustle of her silk down the stairs."

"Have not the pearls been sent yet? Oh, dear, how vexatious!" exclaimed the young lady on entering the room, most elegantly dressed. She seated herself in an affected attitude on the sofa, with a very melancholy expression on her face, as she played with her feather-tipped fan.

"I do believe they are," cried Charles, as a loud ring was heard at the outer bell.

DRESSED FOR THE BALL.

Clementina sprang up eagerly, and hurried to the door—so eagerly, so impatiently, that her little feet tripped, and she fell with some violence to the ground!

CHAPTER XIX.

"OU are not hurt, I hope," exclaimed both cousins, hastening to Clementina's assistance, and raising her; for, in her ball-dress, she was more helpless than ever.

"She is hurt, I fear," cried Ernest, as he saw red drops trickling from her brow, and falling on her lace dress. "Oh, Charles, do call Mrs. Clayton directly."

The lady's maid was instantly summoned, and the hurts of the trembling, sobbing, almost hysterical Clementina examined. She had received rather a deep cut on the forehead, and a little contusion under the eye. There was nothing to alarm, but much to disfigure. Charles proposed sending at once for the doctor, but this the young lady would not hear of: she had some vague, terrible idea, of wounds being sewn up, and much preferred the mild surgery of Mrs. Clayton.

In the midst of the confusion occasioned by the accident, two lamps were seen to stop before the door, and the thundering double rap which succeeded announced the return of Mrs. Hope.

The servant who came to say that his mistress was
waiting, laid at the same time a box on the table : it
contained the much-wished-for pearls.

"I had better go down and tell what has happened,"
said Charles, quitting the drawing-room.   In two or
three minutes he returned with Mrs. Hope.

"My darling child ! my sweet Clemmy ! what a sad
business this is !   How could it have happened ?   Why,
you look as though you had been to the wars ! you will
never be able to go to the ball."

Clementina leaned her head on the sofa, and sobbed
piteously.

"Dear me !   I hope, Clayton, that you have put on
the plaster carefully.   I only dread her being marked
for life," said the mother.

The poor girl's grief became more violent.

"You must compose yourself, my dear ; you will
make yourself ill.   A fall is a great shock to the nerves."

Ernest had left the room as the lady entered, and now
silently offered to his cousin's trembling hand a glass of
sal volatile and water.

"You had better go to bed at once," said Mrs. Hope.
"'Tis such a pity ; all ready dressed for the ball !   I
must go, for I could not disappoint Lady Fitzwigram,
and I believe that the Duchess is to be there.   Clayton
will take excellent care of you, I am sure.   Come, Ernest
and Charles, I see that you are ready."

"And I am to be left all alone, and on this night, just when I expected to be so happy!" sobbed Clementina.

"I should like to stay with her, I should indeed," said Ernest to his aunt; "I hope that you will not object to my doing so."

"Why, what will Lady Fitzwigram say?"

"She will not care; she has never seen me but once. You will be so kind as to make my excuses."

"Well, it is very considerate of you, certainly. I don't know what to say," replied Mrs. Hope, very well pleased to be able to tell a fashionable circle that Lord Fontonore had stayed behind because her daughter could not come. So the matter was soon decided; the carriage moved off slowly with Mrs. Hope and Charles, and Ernest and his weeping cousin were left behind, to spend the rest of the evening quietly together.

Never before had Clementina found her cousin half so agreeable as now. He was so gentle, so considerate, so ready to sympathize with her, that she began suddenly quite to change her opinion of him, and think the young peer a very delightful companion. She had hitherto been rather provoked at his indifference towards her; now, as she had little idea of the nature of Christian courtesy, she attributed all his kindness to admiration. She thought that the white bandage across her brow might have an "interesting" effect; and Ernest's gentle consideration would have lost half its power to please, had Clementina been aware that it would have been equally shown to one in a humbler class of life of the age of forty instead of fourteen.

As she reclined on the sofa, and Ernest sat beside her, it was a great comfort to her to be able to pour out her

CLEMENTINA AND ERNEST.

complaints to him. "There never was anything so unfortunate," said she; "you can't imagine what it is to have such a disappointment."

"I think that I can, Clementina, for I was once most bitterly disappointed myself."

"Oh, but you are such a sober creature, such a philosopher. I daresay that you scarcely gave it a thought."

"On the contrary, I felt myself almost overwhelmed. I could hardly speak, I could hardly keep from tears."

"You!" exclaimed Clementina in surprise.

"I thought," continued Ernest, "that there was no one on earth so unhappy as I—that all happiness in this world was gone."

"What could have made you so wretched?" cried the girl, her curiosity so much roused that her own troubles were for the moment forgotten.

"I had lost what I greatly desired."

"And what could that have been, Ernest?"

"A situation so much below my real rank, that I smile now to think that I could ever have wished for it. Had no difficulties been in my way, had I had what I desired, I probably never should have possessed my birth-right. How glad I am now of what so much distressed me then!"

"And what was it you were so miserable at losing?"

"A place in the service of Mr. Searle."

"You don't say so!" exclaimed Clementina, opening her eyes to their widest extent. "That was below you indeed; what an escape you made!"

"Perhaps nothing that ever happened to me caused me more pain."

"Oh! that was because you did not know what you really were, or you would have looked a good deal higher."

"Now, Clemmy, it seems to me that this is the very reason why you are so unhappy this evening."

"What! that I do not know what I really am? what can you mean!" exclaimed the girl, yet more astonished than before.

"If you discovered that you were a king's daughter, would you fret for a ball, or care for a blow?"

"Really, Ernest," cried Clementina, half curious, half inclined to think him jesting, though he did not look so, "I wish you would speak so that I could understand you."

"I wish you to look higher, dear cousin; you set your thoughts and your hopes too low, on things far more beneath your real station and privileges than the office of a servant was beneath mine. Are you not the child of the King of kings; is not a mansion in heaven offered to you; may not the white robes and golden crown be preparing for you now; and yet you seem as though you knew not of the bliss set before you—you are content to be a servant?"

"To whom?" interrupted Clementina.

"To the world; and oh, my cousin, the world is a bad master! you have tasted this night what wages it can give; God grant that you know not much more of their bitterness hereafter."

"Why, Fontonore, what is the matter? why do you speak so?" cried Clementina, looking half frightened at her cousin's earnest face; for it cost him no small effort to address her thus, and he warmed with his own words as they flowed on.

" I speak thus because I long to see you happy, really happy. Now you are only, as it were, blowing bubbles of pleasure: you touch them and they break, and are gone for ever. Oh, let us seek that which is lasting and sure—that which will be ours when these frail bodies are dust."

" It is very unkind in you to talk of such things to me when I am weak and nervous, it makes one so horribly gloomy."

"Does it make one gloomy to hear of sins being pardoned ; does it make one gloomy to hear of a Father in heaven ; to know that treasures are laid up for us where neither moth nor rust can corrupt, where happiness is as lasting as it is perfect. Did it make me gloomy to hear that I had a rich inheritance."

" Oh, that was quite a different thing ! " cried Clementina, " from becoming one of your pious saints. You talk to me now only about happiness in religion, but I know very well all the lectures upon holiness, and unworldliness, and repentance that will follow."

" Still my comparison holds," pursued the young peer, " for I have not yet entered into full possession of my estate ; I have yet many a difficult lesson to learn, nor can I spend but a portion of what is my own."

" You have a good deal of enjoyment in the meantime."

" I have, Clementina, and in this, most of all, may my

position be compared to a Christian's. He has great enjoyment, pure, present enjoyment, a beginning of his pleasures even here. Does not the Bible command us to rejoice without ceasing?—who can rejoice if the Christian does not? Yes," continued Ernest, his eyes sparkling with animation, "how very, very happy those must be who have gone a long way on their pilgrimage, when I, who am only struggling at the entrance, can say that I have found no pleasure to equal it! Oh, Clementina! my joy when I heard that I was raised from being a poor peasant, forced to toil for my bread, to become one of the nobles of the land—the joy which I felt then was as nothing compared to my delight when I first felt assured that my sins were forgiven me."

Clementina made no reply, and soon after expressed her wish to retire to rest. Those who have never known the happiness of religion find it difficult to believe that it really bestows any. A blind man cannot understand the beauty of light, nor the man deaf from his birth the delight of music. Yet music and light are around us still, and such to the soul is "the joy of the Lord."

"Perhaps some day she may reflect over what has passed," thought Ernest, as he bade his cousin a courteous good-night; "and at least one thing is left that I can do for her still—I will never cease to pray."

CHAPTER XX.

"Now at the further side of that plain was a little hill, called Lucre, and in that hill a silver mine."—*Pilgrim's Progress.*

EXT morning Charles came down to breakfast late, after his party. Clementina did not make her appearance at all. In answer to Ernest's question, as to whether he had enjoyed himself, Charles answered quickly, "Very much indeed;" and added, that he was going to meet the Fitzwigrams again that day, at the house of a mutual friend.

"I am sorry that you are to be absent another evening from me," said Ernest; and as soon as breakfast was concluded he drew Charles aside. "I wonder at your caring to be so much with the Fitzwigrams," said he; "of all our worldly acquaintance they seem to me the most worldly."

"There's charity for you!" laughed Charles.

"I do not wish to be uncharitable, or to judge any one," said Ernest; "but I love you too well to be indifferent as to the friendships that you form. Your whole happiness through life may depend upon your choice."

"Well, I grant you that they are citizens of Vanity Fair; but they are very pleasant people for all that."

"Let us remember, Charles, the test which Mr. Ewart recommended to us, when we are selecting our friends. 'Before you are intimate with any one,' he said, 'consider whether theirs is the society which you would wish to enjoy throughout eternity.'"

"That is a very serious test, indeed; few friendships in the world would stand it. But don't make yourself uneasy about me, Ernest. As we are to be off for Yorkshire on New Year's day, I shall not have time to draw too close with these Fitzwigrams before we leave."

"You are not going out?" said Ernest, as Charles walked towards the stand in the hall on which were placed the gentlemen's hats.

"Yes; I'm going to buy that book for Mr. Ewart. I only hope that I may not find it sold."

"But I thought that you said yesterday that you had not the money for it?"

"Yesterday I had not, but to-day I have. I had then silver in my purse, now I have gold!"

"Have you received anything, then, from our uncle?"

"From him! Oh, no! Do you think that he has a thought to spare from the dissolution of the Parliament, the prospects of the ministry, the progress of the canvass, and all that sort of thing?" said Charles, imitating the pompous manner of Mr. Hope.

"I wish," said Ernest, "I wish that you would tell me where and how you obtained that money. I need hardly say to you, dear Charles, that it is no mean curiosity that makes me ask."

"Well, if you will have the truth of it, I won it last night at the card-table, at Lady Fitzwigram's. There, don't look so grave; I've committed no crime; the money is honestly mine."

"I cannot but look grave," replied Fontonore. "Oh, Charles, if you had but seen what I have seen of gambling! It gave me a feeling of pain, when at Holyby, Ann's poor boys used to play at pitch and toss, and gamble for halfpence; for I beheld in their father how such amusements might end. The love of play, which is the love of gold in one of its most fatal forms, is what first brought Lawless to guilt and ruin. It grew upon him, stronger and stronger, a habit that could not be broken, till I have known him desperately stake his last shilling, with his hungry children around him wanting bread, to gratify this miserable passion; nay, gamble away the very blanket in which his sick little one was wrapped!"

"But I do not lose; I gain."

"Whoever gains, some one must lose; you either receive or inflict a loss."

"I care little about the money," cried Charles; "it is the feeling of excitement that I enjoy."

"And it is in this very feeling that the danger lies. There need be no sin in simply playing a game. I have heard that good Mr. Searle likes his quiet whist, and no doubt he enjoys it with an easy conscience; but when it is not in the game, but in the gambling, that the pleasure is found—when the interest is excited, not by exercise of skill, but by the chance of a lucky deal—oh, Charles, is it not a kind of intoxication which the young Pilgrim especially is bound to shun?"

"There is a sort of intoxication in all sorts of worldly excitement, I think," observed Charles. "The expectation of a ball intoxicates my cousin; the chances of an election, her father; great heroes are intoxicated by a desire for conquest. What was Napoleon but a mighty gambler?"

"Yes," subjoined Ernest; "one who played for kingdoms, and gambled away crown, liberty, and all."

"Well, to me there is something great and animating in the idea of putting it 'to the touch, to gain or lose it all.'"

"If that be your feeling, Charles," exclaimed Fontonore, "you are one who should never touch a card. There is the fuel ready in your heart. Oh, beware of letting a spark fall upon it! How can you pray not to be led into temptation, without mocking the great Being whom you address, if you, with your eyes open, seek the company and the amusements which you know in themselves to be temptation? You would be as one who, because the day was fair and the water inviting, would venture in a boat close to a dangerous whirlpool, and, while he felt the strong current drawing him in, would content himself with praying for some wind from heaven to save him from the peril into which he had thrown himself."

"The difference here," observed Charles, " is, that I can stop when I like."

"Every gambler begins by thinking that he can stop when he likes, till he finds that habit and passion are too strong to be mastered. Oh, Charley! my Charley!" continued Ernest, with emotion, "much as I love you, my own only brother, I had rather lose you—rather see you laid in your grave, than living the life of a gambler!"

"You shall never see me a gambler,—I mean, God helping me," replied Charles, touched and gratified by his brother's anxiety ; "I will give up play after this evening."

"Do not go this evening ; it is playing on the brink of temptation."

"Would you have me break an engagement?"

"You can write, and make your excuse. To-morrow is Christmas day, when we should especially remember the mercy that opened to us the gate of salvation, and our duties as pilgrims and soldiers of the Cross. You would not spend this evening amongst those whom you yourself call citizens of Vanity Fair?"

"I will not write, then; I will call—it is more courteous."

"More dangerous."

"I see that you have little trust in me," said Charles, but without any emotion of anger. "Perhaps, Ernest, you know me better than I do myself: but I think that in this case I only do right to go; therefore it is not wilfully throwing myself into temptation."

Charles found Aleck Fitzwigram at the house of Leo Chamberlain, his friend, and after shaking hands with them both, told them that he had come to say that circumstances would prevent his joining them that evening.

"Then you'll come to-morrow—no, we dine out then, and the day after there's the theatre; but on Saturday, at any rate, we shall expect you here; you know that you must give us our revenge."

Charles took the piece of gold out of his waistcoat pocket, and laid it upon the table. "You will need no revenge," said he, smiling.

"Hope, what do mean by that? This is some jest of yours! You don't want us to think that you are not going to play with us again?"

"I wish you to think the truth."

"Who on earth has put this absurdity into your head?"

Charles would have liked far better if he could have said that no one had put a fear of gambling into his head, but that it was the result of his own reflections on the subject; for one of the causes of our so seldom benefiting by the experience of others, is the pride of the human heart, which hates the idea of being led. But, in the present case, no other truthful answer could be given, and Charles replied, "My brother has made me think differently upon this subject from what I did before."

"Your brother—Fontonore! Well, this is the best joke that ever I heard in my life! You, who have lived from your birth with those who know what life is, to allow yourself to be led by a boy who passed all his early years with tinkers, or ploughmen, or thieves; who is ignorant of all that a gentleman should know, and prudently avoids opening his lips for fear of speaking bad grammar!"

Charles felt more inclined to be angry than to laugh. The arrow fell lightly as regarded his brother's conversation; for whether it was from natural delicacy of mind, or Ernest's more than common acquaintance with the pure language of Scripture, his speech was never coarse, and occasionally, when he overcame his reserve, flowed on in unstudied eloquence, unusual in one so young. Charles was indignant at the unfeeling allusion to the trials of Ernest's early life. "You forget that you speak of my brother," said he.

"He has given you good cause to remember that he is your brother, and your *elder* brother too," said Fitzwigram, with a sneer. "But I should have thought it enough for him to have had my name, my fortune, and my estate, without letting him put my judgment also in his pocket, and not leave me even a will of my own!"

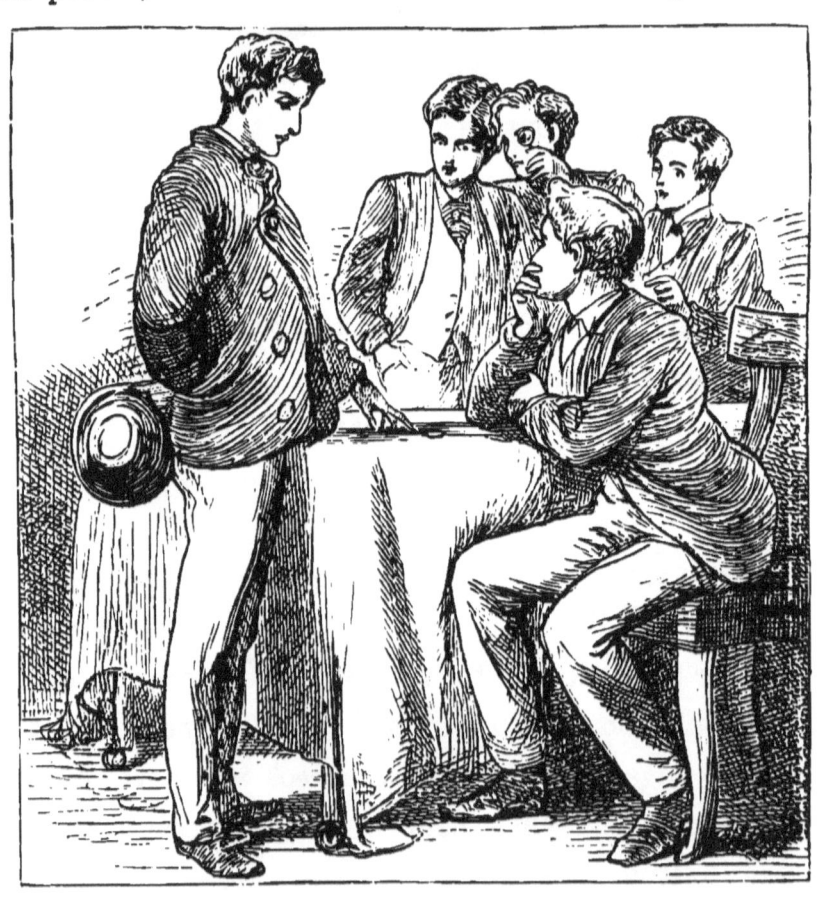

CHARLES AND FITZWIGRAM.

The blood of young Hope mounted to his forehead. He was beset again by the same enemy, Shame, who clung to Faithful in the Valley of Humiliation. To the Pilgrim that valley was not yet passed, that enemy was not yet conquered. But Charles remembered the words of Faithful, which had made a strong impression on his mind : "Shame, depart! thou art an enemy to my salvation. Shall I entertain thee against my sovereign Lord ? How shall I then look Him in the face at His coming ?" With a brave resolve to grapple with his own enemy within, as well as to stand the ridicule of tempters without, Charles replied, that if he adopted the principles of his brother, he should gain from him far more than he had lost ; and bidding a cool farewell to his late companions, he quitted the house more truly a victor than many a hero who has written his title to glory in the blood of his fellow-creatures.

CHAPTER XXI.

GREEN PASTURES AND STILL WATERS.

"I saw then that they went on their way to a pleasant river, which David the king called 'the river of God,' but John 'the river of the water of life.'"—*Pilgrim's Progress.*

N various manners was the succeeding day passed by the different members of Mr. Hope's household. He himself was absent till dinner-time, busy in holding consultations with parliamentary friends. Why should he remember that on that day a Saviour was born into the world? He never considered that he needed one! Lady Fitzwigram called in her carriage for Mrs. Hope, to drive her to a distant church to hear some very famous preacher. Arrayed in all the pomp of Vanity Fair, her mind full of the world, its follies, its ambition, the lady departed to kneel in the house of God, and call herself a miserable sinner! Clementina would have accompanied her mother, but for the disfigurement of her face. Till the bruise had disappeared, and the cut become healed, she could not endure to let herself be seen. So she shut herself up in the drawing-room, with her feet on the fender, listening sadly to the cheerful chime of "the church-going bell," which brought no thought of joy to her heart.

Ernest came into the room, Christmas sunshine on his face. He had not seen his cousin that morning until now.

"A happy Christmas to you, Clemmy, and a joyful New-year."

No look of pleasure on her part responded to the greeting; but she gave the usual answer—"I wish the same to you."

"Thank you. A happy Christmas! I have it. The new year!—ah! how strange it is to think all that a new year may bring!"

"The new year can bring to you nothing so good as the old one has done," said Clementina.

"This year has brought much to me indeed," replied Ernest, thoughtfully. "The Bible—my first knowledge of Mr. Ewart—my brother."

"Oh, your estate, your title!" exclaimed Clementina. "The new year can raise you no higher."

"Only in one way, perhaps."

"And what is that way?"

Ernest did not hear the question of the young lady; his thoughts had wandered to the white marble monument in the church near Fontonore. When we stand on the verge of a new year, and look on the curtain which hides from us the mysterious future, what reflecting mind but considers the possibility that the opening year may to him be the last? To the Christian Pilgrim alone that thought brings no feeling of gloom.

"Are you going to church with us, cousin?" said Ernest, rousing himself from his meditations.

"You had only to look at me to answer your own question," replied the young lady, pettishly. "What could take me to church, with my forehead plastered up and such a yellow mark under my eye?"

Ernest could not help thinking that if she went to church to worship God, and not to be seen of man, there was nothing to keep her away now. But to have expressed his thoughts aloud would have been only to irritate; and the Christian who would lead another to the Lord must be cautious to avoid giving unnecessary offence. There is a time when it is our duty to speak, and a time when it is our wisdom to be silent.

Ernest left the room, and in a few minutes returned with his own copy of the Pilgrim's Progress in his hand. He made no observation, but he laid it near his cousin, and then quitted the house with a secret prayer that the poor girl, to whom religion was as yet but a name, might be led to read, and be guided to understand it.

As the brothers returned from church arm in arm, Ernest felt more than usual joy and peace shed over his spirit: while all was winter without, all was summer within. It was one of those hours which Christians sometimes meet with in their pilgrimage, perhaps as a fore-taste of the bliss that awaits them, when their path appears so bright, and heaven so near, that they feel as though earth's mists were already left behind, and can scarcely believe that they can ever wander again from the way which they find so delightful. They could then lay down their lives with pleasure for their Lord. Life is happiness to them, for in it they may serve Him; and death no object of terror or doubt, for they know that it can but bring them to Him. *Bless the Lord, O my soul; while I live will I praise Him,* is in the thoughts, and not unfrequently on the lips also: for *out of the abundance of the heart the mouth speaketh,* and the heavenly joy which fills all the spirit will sometimes overflow in words.

" O Charley, how joyous the angels' song sounded to-day ! ' *Glory to God in the highest; on earth peace, goodwill toward men.*' What wonder and delight must have filled the hearts of the shepherds when first they listened to that song ! "

" And the angels, it must have made even angels happier to have carried such a message to the world."

" I have sometimes thought," said Ernest, " that if an angel from heaven were to live upon this earth, and to be permitted to choose what station he would fill, he would ask,—not to be a conqueror, not to be a king, not even to be one of the geniuses whose discoveries astonish

the world, but to be one who might constantly be pro-
claiming to all the good tidings of a Saviour's coming,
repeating continually that song of heaven, ' *Glory to God,
good-will toward men !* ' "

" He would be a clergyman, or a missionary, then."

" That is what I should most of all wish to be," said
Ernest, " if I only could be worthy of such an honour."

" Why, you are a lord."

" Were I a prince, what nobler office could I have than
to follow in the steps of the apostles and the martyrs—
nay, the steps of the Saviour himself? To sow seeds
that would blossom in eternity! to be a shepherd over the
Lord's dear flock ! Oh, Charles, can we ever realize the
full extent of that promise, *They that turn many to
righteousness*, shall shine *as the stars for ever and
ever !* "

" I feel afraid to be a clergyman," said Charles, gravely.
" My uncle spoke to me about it yesterday : he said that
the church might be the best opening for me in life, and
that it was time for me to think of a profession. But,
Ernest, there was something that went against my feelings in thinking of it in that light."

" I am sure that you were right, my brother. How
could one dare to become the minister of God from any
other motive than the desire to serve Him, and proclaim
His message to dying sinners around us ? "

" I was afraid that you would blame me. I thought

that you would urge me to devote myself to the service of the ministry."

"Not unless your service were that of the heart; then indeed I should rejoice at your choice. But what are your own wishes for yourself?"

"I have always had rather a fancy for being a soldier. The danger and excitement of the life attracts me. I should like to be just such a warrior as Great-heart, who fought and conquered Giant Despair."

"I thought," observed Ernest, smiling, "that Great-heart was intended to represent a minister, and not a soldier."

"Do you really think so?" said Charles.

"Only consider his office, and the nature of his exploits. Was he not sent to guide feeble pilgrims, and lead them to the heavenly city? Did not his words cheer and help them on the way? Did he not show them the spring at which they drank and were refreshed, and fight the giant Maul, who led young pilgrims into error? Remember his own account of himself, when he said, 'I am a servant of the God of heaven : my business is to persuade sinners to repentance.' Surely this is a description of a minister of the gospel."

"It never struck me so before."

"If you love difficulties," continued Ernest, "who has greater to overcome than a conscientious clergyman? He has the world to oppose him, Satan to oppose him, his own sinful nature, like a traitor within the gates. He is appointed a commander in the army of the Lord."

"And a missionary is the leader of a forlorn hope," interrupted Charles.

"Not *forlorn*," exclaimed Ernest ; "his hope is sure : if faithful, he is certain of both victory and life."

"I believe, after all," said Charles, "that a clergyman's is the noblest, as well as the most anxious of professions. But even did I wish it to be mine, the question remains—Could I ever be worthy of it ?"

"Ah, that is my difficulty too," cried Ernest ; "and yet," he added hopefully, "I cannot but think that He who first gave us a love for the work, would also give us strength to perform it."

By this time the brothers had reached home. Ernest found the drawing-room empty. A novel lay on the table near which Clementina had been sitting, but the Pilgrim's Progress had evidently been moved from the place where her cousin had left it. He remained, like many others who try to do good, in uncertainty as to whether his endeavours had been fruitless; but with the sweet assurance that whether successful or not, the smallest attempt to serve others, for the sake of the Lord, would never be forgotten by Him.

In another week the family returned to Fontonore, whither Mr. Hope had preceded them by a few days in order to carry on his canvass. If the castle was beautiful at the end of autumn, when Ernest first saw his birth-place, not less striking was its appearance now. The red globe of the winter's sun seemed to rest upon the battlements, gleaming faintly on the arched windows crusted with hoar frost. Every twig on the creepers that mantled the walls, every leaf on the evergreens that adorned the entrance, was covered with white glistening crystals, like the work of a fairy enchantress.

On the bridge on which Mr. Ewart had stood to see the boys depart, he again appeared to welcome them back; and nothing gave so much pleasure to their hearts as his warm, affectionate greeting.

Ernest found everything much as he had left it. Ben appeared, indeed, to have somewhat improved under the careful instruction which he had received; but Jack was the same forward, reckless boy, dead to every feeling of gratitude or shame. He was noted in the castle for mischief-making; his word was never to be depended upon ; he seemed to have inherited his father's love for gambling ; but perhaps the most painful feature in his character was his undisguised dislike of his young benefactor.

" I should almost recommend," said Mr. Ewart, when speaking on the subject to his pupil, " that some other situation should be found for this unhappy boy, where he might be under severer control, and less in a position to give annoyance."

"It would certainly be a great relief to me," replied Ernest.

"He might be apprenticed to some trade."

"That would cause some expense," observed Ernest.

"True, but your uncle—"

"Oh, I never would trouble my uncle upon the subject. My own quarter's allowance is now due, but I have spent it already in my mind. You know my little project for a school here: both Jack and Ben would attend that every day. Oh, we must give him a little longer trial; I cannot afford any changes at present without sacrificing things more important."

"But the irritation to yourself," exclaimed Charles, who was present ; "the constant annoyance and worry caused by such a creature as that !"

"These are the little vexations that are sent to try our patience and forbearance," replied Ernest. "If we seek to bear them with a pilgrim's spirit, perhaps we may discover in another world that we have owed more to our enemies than to our friends."

CHAPTER XXII.

"Now, a little before them, there was on the left hand of the road a meadow, and a stile to go over into it, and that meadow is called By-path meadow."—*Pilgrim's Progress.*

H, the interest and the excitement of an election! How little we consider, when we glance over a dry list of the members of the House of Commons, all the efforts and sacrifices that have been made, the anxiety, heartburnings, sleepless nights, exhausting days, that have been endured to place a single name on that list!

Not only the castle, but all the neighbourhood, was in a ferment, for this was to be a hotly contested election. For some years Mr. Hope had quietly sat as member for the adjacent town of Allborough; but it was now known that he must have a desperate struggle for his place—a wealthy, popular man, had come forward to oppose him: Mr. Stacey was the supporter of a very popular measure, and though the truth was scarcely acknowledged at Fontonore, the chances in favour of the pink were considered equal to those in favour of the blue.

Nothing was talked of at the castle, scarcely anything thought of, but the election. Mr. Hope exerted himself as if his life depended upon success ; his lady was, if possible, more anxious than himself, she was so proud of being the wife of an M.P., she thought that it added so much to her dignity in society. Even Clementina employed her delicate fingers with a little more energy than she usually thought " refined," to make up cockades of blue satin ribbon. She wished the colours had been reversed, "as pink is so much more becoming ;" but as her complexion had never been consulted in the choice, she made up her mind to appear in blue.

The boys naturally caught the infection of the time. Charles was wild for the Blues, and accompanied his uncle very often on his canvassing rounds. He felt ready to knock down any one who dared express a doubt of Mr. Hope's success. And though Ernest had suffered too much, and had reflected too much, to be quite so violent in his emotions, besides wanting even the smattering of politics which his brother had naturally picked up, he also took his part with interest in the proceedings, and watched with almost as much pleasure the erection of the polling-booth, covered with gaudy placards of red and blue, on which " HOPE FOR EVER !" and " VOTE FOR STACEY !" appeared in large, staring letters, as he did the conversion of a barn into a little school which he was preparing for the cottagers around.

Sometimes, indeed, the thought would cross the mind of the boy, as he looked on excited faces, and listened to animated conversation on the all-engrossing theme,— " How strange it is that so much more interest is taken in the things of this life than in what regards another ! It is as though pilgrims to the celestial city should exert all their efforts, strain every nerve, to gain possession of some hillock by the way !"

The day before the election was one of those mild bright days which sometimes occur in the midst of winter, like a little green oasis in a desert, to remind us of the spring which is to come. The air felt almost balmy and warm, and Mr. Ewart and his two pupils walked out to enjoy the sweet sunshine in the park. There was a rustic chair beneath one of the fine old trees, on which the clergyman sat down, while the boys, on the other and more sheltered side of the huge tree, amused themselves with gathering and examining some peculiar moss.

Mr. Ewart had scarcely taken his seat when a step was heard on the dry withered leaves with which the turf was thickly strewn. A rough-looking man approached and touched his hat ; Mr. Ewart recognized the butcher who supplied the castle, and in his usual courteous manner, wished Mr. Staines good morning.

The tradesman replied to the salutation, but stood

lingering as if he had something to say, and yet felt difficulty in beginning the conversation.

"Did you wish to speak to me?" said Mr. Ewart, observing his hesitation.

MR. STAINES AND THE TUTOR.

"Why, sir, I have been wishing very much to say a word to you about to-morrow's election."

"You must be aware," replied the clergyman, "that I make it my rule to take no part in politics."

" I wished to consult you, sir,—"

" I must decline giving advice on these subjects."

" But, sir, it is a matter of conscience !"

" If so, then I am ready to hear you."

" As you of course know, sir," said the butcher, rubbing his head, " Mr. Hope expects me to give him my vote. I have the custom of the castle here, and that's a great matter for a man like me. But you see, sir,"—he stopped and scraped the ground with his foot, then, as the clergyman waited patiently for the rest of his speech, continued with a good deal of embarrassment,—" you see I think all the other way from Mr. Hope, and I did promise to vote for Mr. Stacey."

" Then what brings you now to me ? You cannot be ignorant that in my position as tutor to Lord Fontonore, this is a most delicate affair for me to interfere in."

" I know it, I know it, sir," said the tradesman, lowering his voice ; " but I have never received from any person in the world the advice that I have received from you. A man needs good counsel, you see, at a pass like this, when one is afraid of going against a customer on the one hand, and—and—conscience upon the other."

" Conscience before interest always," said Mr. Ewart.

" You don't mean that I should vote against Mr. Hope?" cried the butcher, who perhaps secretly wished that the tutor of the candidate's nephews might find some means

of relieving his scruples, or take on himself the responsibility of silencing them at once.

"Do ever what is right, and leave the event to a
higher hand," replied the clergyman, rising to conclude
so annoying an interview, and motioning to the tradesman to leave him.

"My uncle would not thank you for your counsel,"
said Charles, coming forward as soon as the voter had
departed.

"I hope that he may never know of it," subjoined
Ernest; "he would be wounded in his tenderest point."

"I much regret that I was consulted," said Mr. Ewart,
gravely; "but, being so, I do not see what other answer
I could have given."

"Oh, you did right, as you always do!" exclaimed
Charles; "but I hope that that vote may not lose us
the election—it would be almost enough to drive one
wild."

There was a sudden change in the weather before the
next morning dawned: the snow was falling fast,
mantling the earth with white; the sky was of one dull
gray; the wind shrieked through the leafless branches.
It was a day when it might have been imagined that no
one would have willingly quitted a warm hearth to face
the inclemency of the weather; yet no one in Castle
Fontonore seemed to regard either frost, wind, or snow.

There were banners flying, bands playing, crowds gathering, the tramp of horses, and the noise of shouting. The snow that fell so soft and white became hardened and brown beneath the hurried tread of many feet. To the poll, from the poll — on horseback, on foot — eager messengers crossed each other, to rouse wavering partisans to exertion, or carry tidings to eager listeners.

The candidates had been proposed, their speeches had been made; all that now remained was for the voters to hasten to the poll. Great was the excitement in the castle when, at the end of the first hour, the statement of numbers was brought in. Mrs. Hope stood flushed and panting with anxiety, and looked half surprised, half mortified, to hear that her husband was but *thirteen* ahead of his opponent.

The next hour his success appeared yet more doubtful — the thirteen had diminished to *seven*. Then again Mr. Hope's majority rose; and his lady, as if assured of triumph, glanced proudly around and repeated for the hundredth time her assertion that she had never for a moment doubted of victory.

Ernest and Charles rode on their ponies amidst the gathered crowds. Every cheer that rose as the Lord of Fontonore and his bright-haired young brother appeared, with large blue cockades on their breasts, seemed a pledge of the success of their uncle.

At length the eventful moment for the close of the

poll drew near.   Mrs. Hope could hardly endure to
await the result in the castle ; but such was the desire
of her husband.   Restlessly she paced up and down the
hall, starting at every sound, watching with breathless
anxiety for news from the polling-place.   Not that she
would admit that she had the slightest fear of defeat.
It was impossible that Mr. Hope could fail of election,
with his connections, his talents, his standing : she only
wondered at the audacity of his opponent, and stopped
repeatedly, in her impatient walk to and fro, to desire
Ernest to write down the name of some titled friend to
whom she must write by the very first post, to com-
municate the news of her triumph.

"Hark ! that's the sound of a horse's quick tramp,"
exclaimed Ernest, starting to his feet.   "That's Charles,
I am sure.   He brings tidings."   The next moment the
hoofs clattered through the archway, and the rider flung
himself off the saddle, even before the panting animal
stopped at the door.

Mrs. Hope and Ernest hurried to meet him ; but the
eager question died on the lips of the lady, as she saw
the expression on her nephew's face.

"Lost ! all lost !" exclaimed Charles, almost stamp-
ing with impatience ; "lost by a minority of *one !*"

"Impossible !   It cannot be !" cried Mrs. Hope.
"There must be some mistake, or some treachery."

But no ; there was neither treachery nor mistake

Every new-comer confirmed the tidings, and Ernest had an opportunity of again witnessing how heavily disappointment falls on the citizens of Vanity Fair. Would that the citizens of a more glorious place lived so far above the world that its trials should never have power to drag them down to the level of its slaves! Are the trifles which so often ruffle our tempers and depress our spirits worth such anxious thought from those who profess that their hearts and their treasures are above?

Mr. Hope's disappointment, anger, and irritation knew no bounds. He was ill able to afford the expense of a contested election. He had spared no trouble, no exertion, no cost; and to lose it after all, and by a minority of *one*, was more than the worldly man could endure.

Mr. Hope talked over the events of the day with his wife in the evening; Ernest and Charles sitting at a little distance, with the chess-table before them, but too much interested in the conversation to attend to their game. Their uncle spoke in a rapid and excited manner, accusing this person of bribery and that of perjury, and declaring that he would demand a scrutiny.

"I say, Ernest," whispered Charles, in a very low voice, bending towards his brother, so that no one else should hear him, "I would not for ten thousand pounds that our uncle should know of Mr. Ewart's conversation with the butcher."

"Nor I," replied Ernest, in the same tone. "What do you think would happen if he did?"

"Mr. Ewart would be dismissed at once from the castle. I know that Uncle Hope would be glad of an opportunity to do this. I am certain that he dislikes our friend, and so does Aunt Matilda."

"Oh, I hope and trust that he never may know it!" exclaimed Ernest, startled at the idea of such a misfortune—one of the greatest, he felt, which could befall him, for his affection towards his tutor was deep and sincere.

"I am afraid," said Charles, still whispering, "that my uncle will hear something about the affair. He is aware that Staines was the last man to vote, and that he turned the scale against him : and Jones told us that the butcher had been seen yesterday in our park; and my uncle, who was very angry indeed, declared that he would sift the matter to the bottom."

"You make me very uneasy," said Ernest. "What should we say if we were questioned ? You know that we overheard all."

"I wish that we had been anywhere else," cried Charles ; "but I had no idea that the man had come about anything secret. What should we say if we were questioned ?"

"We could not betray our friend. Oh, Charles, if he were to leave us, how could we ever stand firm against all the temptations which we should be certain to meet ?"

" Who would help you to carry out your plans of usefulness ?"

" Who would be our guide in our pilgrimage ?"

" And it might be ruin to Mr. Ewart to be sent away. You know that he supports his aged mother. His voice is not strong enough for severe clerical duty ; he might never be able to get a church."

" I would do anything to prevent such a misfortune happening," cried Ernest.

" *Anything ?* Would you tell an untruth ?"

" In such a case as this, I hardly think that it would be wrong ?"

Charles looked very doubtfully at his brother.

" Why, consider, Charles, all the evil that might follow if my uncle knew the truth—evil to us, to all around us, to our dear friend himself. Nothing should make us swerve from strict candour where only our own interests are concerned ; but when a good man may be ruined—"

Here the conversation was suddenly broken off by Mr. Hope's turning towards them, and exclaiming, in a loud tone,—

" And there's something which you may help me to clear up, young gentlemen. I have heard a rumour—a very strange rumour, one that it is scarcely possible to

credit—that that fellow Staines was hanging about the
park yesterday, and had a consultation with Mr. Ewart,
who advised him to vote against me.   Were you with
your tutor at the time ?"

"We were with Mr. Ewart all the afternoon," replied
Ernest, his heart throbbing very fast.

"We never left him," added Charles, as his uncle
glanced towards him.

"And do you know nothing of this pretended interview, which may have been—which probably is—
nothing but a malicious calumny, a fable ?   Was there
any such conversation held in your presence ?—a thing
almost impossible to conceive."

"No, sir; there was none," replied Ernest, in a low tone.

"None," repeated Charles, looking down and
blushing.

Mr. Hope surveyed them both with a piercing eye.
How uneasy they felt under his glance ! He questioned
them no more, however, but turned round again towards
the fire, and was soon engaged once more in animated
conversation with his wife.

"Have we done right ?" whispered Charles to his
brother.

"I don't exactly know. I hope so, for we acted
from a good motive. We could not have spoken out,
and ruined our friend. I am sure that God will not
severely judge an act of kindness and gratitude."

Ah! vain confidence, how many have you led astray! who judge of the Almighty by their own false ideas, instead of His pure unerring Word! Where do we find in the Bible that any sin, committed from any motive whatsoever, finds indulgence from the God of holiness and truth?

"I do not feel quite easy," murmured Charles.

"Nor I. Yet I hope that we have not really wandered from the way. I hardly see what else we could have done."

The servants now brought in tea and coffee. Clementina, looking tired and out of spirits, came into the drawing-room, and was almost immediately followed by Mr. Ewart.

"Mr. Ewart," exclaimed Mr. Hope, stopping suddenly in what he was saying on perceiving the entrance of the clergyman, and addressing him in a sharp, stern, decided manner, "allow me to ask you one question."

The tutor silently bowed.

"Did you, or did you not, converse yesterday in the park with the butcher Staines?"

"I did do so," replied Mr. Ewart, without hesitation.

Ernest bit his lip, till he almost brought blood.

"Did you, or did you not, advise him to vote against me?" continued Mr. Hope, in a tone of suppressed fury.

"I advised him to vote according to his conscience."

"And you advised these two boys to speak according

to their conscience!" exclaimed Mr. Hope, in a voice that
made the room ring.   " You, the instructor of youth—
you, the pattern of strict morality—you have taught
your pupils to be hypocrites and liars ; you have corrupted their unsuspicious minds—"

   " Sir," said Mr. Ewart, with dignity ; but Mr. Hope
was too furious to listen.

THE DISMISSAL.

   " I say that you have corrupted them—ruined their
principles.   Your conduct to me I could pass over ; but
I cannot leave my nephews one day longer in the hands
of one who would teach them to be hypocrites.   You
leave the castle to-morrow, sir,—"

"Oh, uncle!—Mr. Hope!" cried Ernest and Charles, springing forward, "Mr. Ewart knew nothing of it; it was we—it was I."

"There is no use speaking," cried the indignant candidate. "From your conduct, I must judge of the instructions which you have received. Two of my family to be guilty of deliberate falsehood!—Sir," he continued, turning towards Mr. Ewart, "you have heard my unalterable decision. You quit the castle to-morrow."

Mr. Ewart bowed gravely, and retired to his own apartment, followed by the almost heart-broken boys.

CHAPTER XXIII.

REGRETS, BUT NOT DESPAIR.

" I have a key in my bosom, called Promise, that will, I am persuaded open any lock in Doubting Castle."—Pilgrim's Progress.

"WHAT has occurred? what could your uncle mean by speaking of deliberate falsehood?" said Mr. Ewart, as soon as the three were alone in his room, and the door closed behind them.

Ernest was too much agitated to speak. Charles told in a few words all that had happened, omitting nothing but his brother's greater share in the fault. Mr. Ewart listened with a look of distress on his countenance, which cut both the boys to the soul.

"We meant well," said Charles in conclusion, "but everything has turned out ill."

"You should rather say," observed the clergyman, in a mild but sad tone, "that you meant well, but that you acted ill."

"And you must suffer for our fault," exclaimed Ernest, in bitter grief.

"What I suffer from most is the thought of your fault."

"But that it should be laid at *your* door, you who have never taught us anything but what is right—oh! it is such cruelty, such injustice—"

"Hush," said the tutor, laying his hand upon Ernest's, "not a word must you utter against your guardian; and remember that he had grounds for his indignation."

Ernest leant both his arms upon the table, and bending down his forehead upon them, wept in silence.

"If you leave us on account of this," cried Charles, with emotion, "we shall never be happy again."

"Not so," said Mr. Ewart, soothingly; "though the Christian is commanded to repent, he is forbidden to despair. Experience is precious, though it may cost us dear: it will be worth even the sorrow which you are feeling now, if this lesson is deeply imprinted on your soul, *Never do evil that good may come.*"

"In no case?" inquired Charles.

"In no case," replied the clergyman.—"We show want of faith in the power of the Almighty, if we imagine that He needs one sin to work His own good purposes. We can never expect a blessing on disobedience."

"What I cannot endure," exclaimed Ernest, raising his head, "is to think what the world will say. I know the colouring that my uncle will put upon the affair—how my aunt will talk to her fashionable friends. She will speak of the danger of evil influence, of her anxiety for her dear nephews, and the shock which it had been to her to find what principles had been instilled into their minds.   Oh, Mr. Ewart, best, dearest friend, we have injured you indeed—we have brought disgrace upon your spotless character ! "

"God knows my innocence in regard to you," replied the clergyman ; "to Him I commit my cause.   To be the object of unjust accusation has often been the appointed trial of His servants.   He can make even this affliction work for their good.   And now, my dear boys, leave me.   I have letters to write, little preparations to make, and I need a brief space for reflection."

" Do you forgive us ? " said Charles, pressing his tutor's hand with a mixture of affection and respect.

"Forgive you ! you have erred but through kindness towards me.   I have nothing to forgive, dear Charles."

Ernest rushed from the room without uttering a word.   Charles followed him through the long corridor, down the broad oaken staircase, to the drawing-room, in which the family was still assembled.

Ernest came to confess, to plead, to entreat ; and he pleaded, he entreated, with the fervent eloquence of one who thinks his whole happiness at stake.   Mr. Hope

THE CONFESSION AND ENTREATY.

listened with a rigid, unmoved look ; his lady, who sat
at her desk, observed, with an unpleasant smile, that the
reverend gentleman had been evidently working upon
the feelings of his pupils.   She interrupted Ernest's
most passionate appeal, by telling that she was at that
moment engaged in writing to her friend, Lady Fitzwigram, about a very superior tutor, of whom she had
spoken to her when in London.   "If Mr. Sligo should
be still disengaged," observed the lady, "this affair may
prove really a fortunate occurrence."

Fontonore and Charles left the room in despair.

Bitterly reproaching themselves for having wandered from the right path, they retired to the chamber of the former, where they both remained for the remainder of the night, for companionship in sorrow was their only consolation in this time of bitter distress.

"It was I who led you into this trouble," cried Ernest. "I have been your tempter, your false guide; all that has happened has been owing to me! How could I ever dare to call myself a pilgrim, after all that has happened, after all the lessons which I have received, to fall away thus, and disgrace my profession! Will not Clementina look upon me as a hypocrite. I could speak to her of the joy of the Lord, of the pleasures of devotion, of the glories of heaven! Ah, how different will she think my actions to my words! She may even place my errors to the account of my religion; my sin will be a stumbling-block in her way."

"Ernest, brother, you must not give way thus. To fall once may not be to fall for ever. God is merciful and ready to forgive; it is foolish, it is wrong to despair."

Poor Charles endeavoured to give comfort, which he much needed himself; yet his grief was not so deep as his brother's. Ernest felt more strongly, what every Christian should feel, that he who has confessed religion openly before men should, above all others, be watchful over his own conduct. The world is ready, is eager to find faults in such; to excuse its own errors by those of God's children ; to accuse of inconsistency, and even of hypocrisy, those who profess to live by a higher standard. Alas, the sins and failings of sincere Christians have done more injury to the cause of the religion which they love than all the open attacks of its enemies !

Ernest was also, perhaps, the most warmly attached to his tutor. Mr. Ewart had been his friend at a time when he had no other : it was through him that he had discovered his right to an earthly title; it was through him that he had learned to hope for a heavenly one; and to have been the means of inflicting deep injury on his benefactor wrung the spirit of the boy with anguish, even greater than the pang of parting with his friend.

Long after Charles, weary and sad, had dropped asleep, Ernest lay awake, revolving bitter thoughts in his mind, almost too miserable even to pray. Never in the course of his whole life of trial had he passed so wretched a night. The envied Lord of Fontonore, in his magnificent castle, surrounded by all that could minister to his ease, was more wretched than Mark Dowley had been in his cottage, hungry, despised, and persecuted. Such are the pangs of a wounded conscience—such the misery of a backsliding professor !

Ernest fell asleep at last, worn out by the conflict in his own mind, and awoke in the morning with a weight on his heart which painfully oppressed, even before he was sufficiently roused to remember what it was that had caused it.

Mr. Ewart did not appear at breakfast, and neither of the boys could taste the meal. The sound in the court-yard of the wheels of the carriage which was to take their tutor away, and the sight of the neat black trunk, labelled and corded, placed ready by the door in the hall, made their hearts feel almost ready to burst.

The family of Mr. Hope avoided being present, but a number of the servants assembled to witness the departure of one who was respected by all. Even Jack and Ben were seen loitering on the drawbridge; and Lord Fontonore could not help remarking that the former surveyed him with a look of even greater insolence than was his wont; but poor Ernest was too much humbled, too much depressed, to be roused to any feeling of anger.

Mr. Ewart came forth, looking pale and thoughtful, but he smiled as soon as he saw his late pupils, and held out a hand to each. He bade a kind farewell to the numerous attendants, with a word of advice or encouragement to some. There were aprons lifted to tearful eyes, saddened looks, and murmured blessings, as the clergyman passed through the assembled throng to where the carriage was waiting. The boys grasped his hands, and kept them within their own, reluctant to unloose that last, firm clasp. He gave them his earnest, solemn blessing, and bade them put their trust in Him who would never leave or forsake them.

"Shall we ever meet again?" faltered Ernest.

"I hope so—I believe so," replied Mr. Ewart, cheerfully. "This very morning I received a kind invitation from Mr. Searle. If I see no other opening before me, I may possibly visit Silvermere early in the spring; and if so—"

"Oh, if you were at the other end of the world, we should find some means of meeting," exclaimed Charles.

"There is one comfort which we may always make our own, when parting from those whom we love," said the clergyman, struggling to keep down his emotions; "all pilgrims travelling the same road come to the same rest at last; though circumstances and distance may divide them here, they may look forward in sure hope to a meeting in heaven."

And he was really gone!—the friend whom Ernest had loved, the guide whom he had followed, the stay upon which he had leaned—all was like a painful, bewildering dream. Again the young peer hastened to his chamber, threw himself on his bed, and vainly sought for the relief of tears. He was roused by feeling an arm thrown round his neck, and looking up, saw Charles, whose flushed face and reddened eyes bore evident traces of weeping.

"Leave me, Charley," he cried; "the sight of your sorrow only makes mine harder to bear. We can never,

never bring back the past. We can never recall the friend whom we have lost. I feel almost in despair."

Charles uttered no reply. Perhaps he could hardly have trusted his voice to make one; but he laid his open Bible on the pillow before Ernest, and silently pointed to the words in Jeremiah: "*Return, ye backsliding children, and I will heal your backslidings. Behold, we come unto Thee, for Thou art the Lord our God.*"

"Oh, Charley!" said Ernest, with emotion, "this is the second time that you have opened the door of hope to your brother!"

"When did I ever do so before?"

"When a poor desolate boy stood beneath a yew-tree, and watched crowds going into the church which he was almost afraid to enter. You came to him then, and said a few simple words, which roused and encouraged at that time; and often since, when I have felt low and fearful, I have repeated those words to myself, 'You must not stay outside.' I have thought of these words as applying to the gate of mercy open to all. Oh, Charley! what a good, what a generous brother you have been to me! Many in your place would have hated and despised me, taunted me with my ignorance and with my early life; but you, even at a time when I have done you great wrong, when I have deprived you of your friend, even led you into sin, you come to comfort and to cheer me;—ever faithful, ever hopeful, ever dear!"

CHAPTER XXIV.

" Beware of the flatterer. As is the saying of the wise man, so we have found it this day, 'A man that flattereth his neighbour, spreadeth a net for his feet' (Prov. xxix. 5)."—*Pilgrim's Progress.*

T was some time before Ernest could regain his usual cheerfulness; constant occupation was what, perhaps, had the most effect in restoring it. Not only did he turn with ardour to his studies, bending all the powers of a most intelligent mind to master the difficulties of learning, but he was never idle in his hours of leisure ; and so well employed his time, that Charles once observed, with a smile, that the sands in his hour-glass were all of gold !

We are commanded to *let* our *light so shine before men, that they may see* our *good works, and glorify* our *Father which is in heaven.* The light of the young Lord of Fontonore shone brightly, enlightening some and cheering many. Until his little school could be finished, he assembled the poor children in an outhouse of the

castle, and not only contributed, almost beyond his
power, to pay the salary of a schoolmaster, but himself
assisted in the task of tuition, and spoke to the little
ones with such heart-fervour of the duties of a pilgrim
and the love of the Saviour, that the cottagers said that
the children never learned so much as when the young
lord himself was their teacher.   Ernest was often to be
seen beneath the widow's lowly roof: he would carry to
the sick poor little comforts from his own table, and
none knew how often he went without pleasures to himself, that he might afford to help those who needed his
assistance.   Large as was his allowance, his charity so
drained it that self appeared almost forgotten ; and the
Lord of Fontonore was scarcely ever known to purchase
anything for his own gratification.   It was his habit, his
privilege, his delight, to lay his treasures at the feet of
his Lord; and thus, though the possessor of great
wealth, the pilgrim pressed on, unclogged and unburdened
by it.

Nor, in attending to the wants of the poor, did Ernest
neglect his home duties. The affection between him and
his brother was a source of happiness to both, and appeared to grow stronger every day ; and Ernest sometimes ventured to hope that he might in time exert a
slight influence even on the frivolous mind of Clementina.   She was, quite unconsciously to herself, less inclined to utter words of folly or ill-nature when in the

presence of her cousin, and felt the quiet glance of his eye a greater restraint than a serious reproof from another. At a time when she suffered from weakness in her eyes, Ernest, busy as he was, seemed always to find time to read to her and amuse her : the book was sometimes her choice, but more often his ; and he gradually led the weak, worldly girl, to take some interest in his favourite Pilgrim.

It may well be imagined that Ernest became exceedingly beloved in the castle. His uncle, indeed, called him an enthusiast, and Mrs. Hope complained that he was too much of a missionary ; but what she would have ridiculed in any one else, she had great indulgence for in a peer. There was but one being, of all those who lived at Fontonore, who seemed rooted in dislike towards the young lord ; and that was the envious, insolent Jack Lawless, whom no benefits softened, no kindnesses won.

I must not omit to mention the arrival of Mr. Sligo, the new tutor, who came to Fontonore about ten days after the departure of Mr. Ewart. Seldom has a new instructor been introduced to his pupils under greater disadvantages as regards their feelings.

" I am certain that I shall dislike him," said Charles to his brother the evening before Mr. Sligo made his appearance. " It will seem to me as though he usurped the place of my friend.

THE NEW TUTOR.

"I confess that I feel a prejudice against any tutor recommended by Lady Fitzwigram.   But then such a prejudice may be neither kind nor just : he never taught in her family, therefore has nothing to do with any of the faults of her sons. We must meet Mr. Sligo in a fair, candid spirit. Mr. Ewart would have been the first to tell us to treat our new tutor as we would wish to be treated in his position ourselves."

Mr. Sligo proved quite a different kind of person from what his pupils had expected. Instead of a proud, opinionative scholar, bearing the stamp of one familiar with the *haut ton*—a walking peerage, a follower of the world and its fashions—they beheld a mild-looking, delicate little man, with a manner quick but gentle, who spoke in low, soft tones, with an almost timid air, as if afraid of giving offence. To such a person it was impossible for a generous spirit to be unkind. The brothers did all in their power to put him at his ease; and they were flattered by the grateful, deferential manner, in which he received the smallest attention. Mr. Sligo was soon found to be not only an intelligent tutor, but a very agreeable companion. He was ready for anything, either business or play; could do anything, from setting a drawing for Charles to assisting in the construction of the school: he entered with pleasure into every project, especially such as had charity for their object, listened to pious sentiments with an approving smile, and delighted in helping forward every good work.

With such a companion, with such occupations and such encouragements, was not our pilgrim almost at the gate of heaven?

Had Ernest been an angel, free from human frailty, perhaps it might have been so with him now. Never had he walked onwards with a firmer step, never had he been such a blessing to others, never had he kept his lips more pure, nor been more watchful over every action; and yet he was, perhaps, in more danger of falling than when passing through Vanity Fair! To a mind like his, the society of a worldly companion might have been less dangerous than that of Mr. Sligo. And why so? His tutor never taught him evil, never set him an evil example. But there was silent flattery in his admiring look, the attention with which he listened, the heartiness with which he approved. With all his quickness of perception, there was one thing which he seemed to lack— the power of discovering a fault in his pupil.

Ernest had endured, without injury, the flattery of the world—he attributed it all to his title. The praises of Charles had nothing dangerous in them—he set them down to a brother's partiality; but it was something new to him to be admired for the very qualities for which, a few months before, he had suffered persecution; it was something delightful to be looked up to by so many, and viewed as a model of Christian benevolence! We may wonder that, after his last sad fall, Ernest could have entertained a thought of spiritual pride; but our enemy is ever watchful and insidious and human nature infirm. We do not willingly dwell upon what gives us pain ; and often, too often, deceive our own hearts from the pleasure which it gives us to be thus deceived.

Ernest had often remarked, that the worldly are constantly engaged in raising pedestals on which to elevate self; he had seen the ambitious build his of popular applause ;—such was Mr. Hope's, and it had crumbled into dust. The proud woman had raised herself by fashion, the vain beauty by the admiration of society. But while Ernest could thus observe the failings of others, he would have been startled and alarmed indeed had he known that he was now raising such a pedestal himself! His very prayers, his alms, his good works, were turned into a stumbling-block in his path ; whatever exalts *self*, stands between us and the Saviour, and we are never safe but when our pride lies humbled in the dust before Him.

I would especially direct the attention of my reader to this last most subtle device of Satan to keep back the pilgrim from heaven. As God draws good out of evil, Satan draws evil out of good, and sometimes makes us deem ourselves most near the celestial city when we are actually turning our faces from it. The most experienced pilgrims may be taken in this snare ; the most zealous, the most devoted Christians are perhaps in the greatest danger from it. We are so ready to forget when the mirror shines brightly, that it is in itself but dust and ashes, borrowing all its radiance from heaven.

The tender leaves were now beginning to appear on the shrubs, and the dark branches of the trees were spangled with the light green buds which told the approach of spring.   The crocus lifted its golden cup from the sod, and the snow-drop trembled on its slender stem. On the day when Ernest would complete his thirteenth year, his school-house was to be opened for the first time.   A number of friends were asked to be present on the occasion,—Mr. Searle, his daughter, and a son from college amongst the rest, Ernest's often-expressed wish having at length overcome the reluctance of his aunt to invite them.   There was to be a band and a collation in honour of the occasion; and the children were abroad early in the sunny morning to gather flowers to decorate the school-room.

The spirits of the young Lord Fontonore rose high, there was so much to gratify and elate him.   Never had he more admired his beautiful home, or more rejoiced in the power to do good.   Mr. Sligo had written an ode to celebrate the day, in which flattery was so delicately mingled with truth, that it could hardly fail to gratify and please.

One by one the company assembled, each with a kind wish or well-turned compliment.   Ernest was of course the hero of the day; and as everything in the school-house was now prepared, the tide of silk and velvet, feathers and lace, moved on towards the little edifice.

The school children lined the path on either side, in clean frocks, with nosegays of wild-flowers in their hands, their ruddy little faces beaming with pleasure at the thought of their expected feast. Passing between the lines, with feelings of natural pleasure, perhaps not quite unmingled with pride, Lord Fontonore, accompanied by his guests, proceeded to the door, which he unlocked and threw open. In a few minutes the school-room was filled. It had been decorated with a good deal of taste by the school children under Mr. Sligo's direction, and Charles had fastened two blue banners above the entrance. There were books for school use judiciously selected, maps on a large scale hung round the room; but every eye in the gay assembly was at once directed to a large black board hung over the fire-place. This was designed for the use of classes in arithmetic, as sums or figures could be chalked upon it of a size to be seen by the whole school. But it was neither sum nor diagram upon it now that drew the attention of every one present, but a coarse sketch, evidently chalked by an untutored hand, though not wanting in spirit or fun, of a boy sitting astride on the top of a wall, with a gigantic peach in his grasp ; and as the picture might not be understood by all, beneath it was written, in a round schoolboy hand, legible from the furthest end of the room, " *The pious Lord Fontonore robbing Farmer Joyce.*"

Ernest was taken by surprise, when quite off his
guard; insulted and exposed in the very hour of his
triumph, and he needed not the sight of Jack's insolent
face at the door to tell him by whom.   A few months
before, he would have struck the boy to the earth; now
the feelings of the Christian, perhaps the dignity of the
noble, prevented any such violent display of his anger;
but he clinched his hand, and with an expression of
fierceness in his flashing eye, which no one present but
the offender himself had ever seen on his countenance
before, Ernest exclaimed in a voice of fury, "Insolent
liar, this is your work!"

A scene of brief confusion ensued.   Mr. Sligo sprang to
the obnoxious board, and in a few moments every trace
of the sketch was removed; but the impression which it
had left on the spectators was not so readily taken away.

"This comes of bringing up such a wolf's cub!" exclaimed Mrs. Hope.

"What an extraordinary piece of impertinence," said
the baronet, on whose arm she leaned.   "Surely," he
added, in a lower tone, "such a story had never any
foundation in truth."

Some recommended a severe thrashing to the offender,
some that he should at once be turned adrift on the
world.   Ernest felt the whole subject intolerably painful;
annoyed as he was at Jack, he was more annoyed at
himself for having been overcome by sudden passion.

Charles, with the quick eye of affection, read his wish in his look; and springing on the table to raise himself above the throng, he began an extempore questioning of the children, conducting his examination with so much spirit and fun as quite to change the current of general conversation.

But though the disagreeable subject was dropped and apparently forgotten, the schoolroom duly admired, and the children's progress applauded, every word of praise and compliment now fell flat upon the ear of Fontonore. The discipline had been bitter, but it was just what he had required. A veil had been suddenly drawn from his eyes; he had been thrown from his pedestal of pride. He had been reminded of what he had been, what he had done, and shown what he still continued to be—a weak, infirm child of dust, subject to passion and sin, having nothing whereof he could boast.

"I was not only angry," thought Ernest to himself, "but uncandid. I gave an impression to all who heard me that I denied that of which I was accused. He who but declared unpleasant truth, in my passion I called a liar. Oh! how greatly have I of late been deceiving myself when believing my conduct to be more consistent than that of others. One thing, however, remains to be done. I can yet make some amends; and I will do so, whatever it may cost my feelings, however it may wound my pride."

As he showed his guests over the castle and grounds, Fontonore was remarkably silent and absent. Charles wondered to himself that the insolence of a boy should have such an effect upon his brother; but he did not guess what deeper feelings were stirring in the breast of the pilgrim. At last Ernest, as if in reply to some question from Clementina, whose sound had fallen upon his ear, but whose sense he had not taken in, proposed that they should all go and see the children at their feast on the lawn.

"I should have thought that we had had enough of those children," said Clementina, with affectation. "I cannot conceive the pleasure of watching them eating, and our presence can be nothing but a restraint."

Towards the lawn, however, the whole party moved, where a long table had been laid out by Ernest's desire, well furnished with a comfortable meal. Sounds little befitting a scene of mirth were heard as the visitors approached. The schoolmaster, who presided at the top of the table, was in an angry indignant voice denying to Jack the right of sitting at it, after openly insulting the provider of the feast. The general feeling of the children ran in the same current; some were loudly calling out, "Shame, shame, turn him out!" But Lawless, with his own insolent self-assurance, appeared inclined to defy them all.

At the appearance of Fontonore and the ladies there

was a sudden silence, and all the party at the feast turned towards him to decide the disputed question. Ernest walked firmly up to the head of the table, very pale, for what he had resolved to do went sorely against human nature; and few efforts are so painful as to trample down pride, and humble ourselves in the sight of the world.

"Let him sit down," said Ernest to the schoolmaster

THE APOLOGY.

The children silently made room for their companion. "Jack Lawless," continued the peer, turning towards the boy, and speaking rapidly, whilst he could not raise his own eyes from the ground, "I regret that I unjustly

called you a liar ; I recall the word now before all who
heard it."

Nothing can describe the astonishment of the whole
assembly as they listened to this apology from the young
lord.   " Brave boy, well done !   He's a soldier that will
not flinch ! " muttered old Mr. Searle, with cordial appro-
bation.

" He must be wild," exclaimed Mrs. Hope, " to expose himself so before a company like this !   To acknowledge such a fact !   Why, I would rather have died than
have disgraced myself so before the world ! "   The lady,
however experienced in the concerns of this life, in
spiritual things was more ignorant than a child, or she
would have known that disgrace is in the commission of
a fault, but never in the frank avowal of it.

CHAPTER XXV.

" Now I saw in my dream, that by this time the pilgrims were entering
into the country of Beulah."—*Pilgrim's Progress.*

HE painful incident recorded in the last chapter
had been to Ernest one of the most instructive
events of his life, and the young lord felt that
it was so.   He recognized the parental care of
his heavenly Father, in openly rebuking his pride ; and
was now so well aware of the peculiar dangers that attended his position, and how much they were increased
by the weak indulgence of his preceptor, that he heard
almost without regret, on the following day, that having
come into some property by the will of a relative, Mr.
Sligo was about to resign his present charge.

Oh, how gladly would Fontonore have recalled his
first friend, him whose love was too sincere for flattery !
This, however, was a thing quite beyond his hopes, and
the boys tried to content themselves with the thought
that they might soon have the pleasure of seeing their
late tutor.   Mr. Searle had told Ernest, when he met

him at the castle, that he expected Mr. Ewart on a visit;
and though the young peer knew that the clergyman
would not come to Fontonore, as such a step might be
displeasing to his uncle, he determined to go over himself to Silvermere, as soon as he should hear that his
friend had arrived there.

One bright, lovely spring morning, with this idea on
his mind, Ernest sauntered forth in the direction of Mr.
Searle's house.   Very beautiful was the scenery which
lay between—so beautiful that the spot was often visited
by strangers, who came from many miles round to see it.

A small lake, so small that we might better term it a
pool, lay embosomed in high rocks, that hung over it as
though to look at their rough crags reflected in its
mirror.   From this beautiful little piece of water, sleeping in their dark shadow, was fed a rapid stream, that,
rushing onward, as if weary of its tranquil repose, made
its way for some short distance through an opening in
the rocks, and then flinging aloft showers of spray, fell
with a bold leap over some lower crags into a wider lake
in the valley below.   There was a wooden bridge over
this stream, some way above the cascade, and on this
bridge Ernest had often delighted to take his station,
where, on the right hand, he could see the quiet upper
lake, so carefully sheltered and guarded from the wind
by the tall rocks that towered around it; on the left,
the wider sheet which lay outspread far below to receive

the rivulet which flowed beneath his feet. It was a lovely spot, and a favourite haunt of one who loved to look up through nature unto nature's God. Ernest thought of the current of human life as he watched the waters bursting forth from the secluded, shady pool, rolling for some brief minutes through a narrow, darkened chasm ; then, as they emerged into the sunny light, plunging with a deep and sudden fall to mix and lose themselves in the brighter waters that lay glittering in the vale.

It was some time now since Ernest had visited this scene, and this morning he felt inclined to bend his steps thither. He feared that his constant round of occupations—his studies, even his charitable pursuits—had made him of late too much neglect that quiet communing with God and his own heart, which should be a pilgrim's privilege and delight. Ernest, therefore, did not ask even Charles to accompany him ; peaceful meditation on the highest subjects that can engage the mind is best enjoyed, is perhaps only enjoyed, in solitude and seclusion.

Ernest was tranquilly, but deeply happy. His discovery of his infirmity had served rather to humble than to depress him. If he had less confidence now in himself, he had more than ever in his Saviour ; and what sweet security came with the thought that it was on no arm of flesh that he rested ! He who had loved him would love to the end. *This God is our God for ever and ever, He will be our guide unto death.*

With holy and happy thoughts for his companions, Fontonore wandered to the little bridge.   It struck him, before he set his foot upon it, that it looked decayed and injured by the weather.   He stooped down to examine the rough timber, between the chinks of which he could see the stream flowing darkly and rapidly by.   A very brief survey strengthened his suspicion that the bridge was in a dangerous state.

" I will not attempt to cross it," said Ernest to himself, " though it is the nearest way to Silvermere.   I must speak to Mr. Searle, and have it repaired.   I think that the property belongs to him.   The long winter has made the wood decay ; and yet, from a little distance, it looks safe and beautiful as ever.   To rest our hopes of heaven upon our works, however fair in man's eyes they might appear, would be like trusting our safety to that frail timber, and first learning our danger by our fall."

Before he quitted the spot, Ernest wished to climb to the top of the highest crag that rose above the cataract, as he from thence would command a view over Silvermere : perhaps he might even see Mr. Ewart in the distance.   The path which led to the height was very narrow and winding, encumbered with thicket and difficult of access, but the prospect from the summit more than repaid all the trouble of the ascent.   An expanse of beautiful country spread around : here cattle were grazing in hedge-bordered fields of emerald velvet spangled with buttercups and daisies ; there stretched woods, clad in the light garb of spring, whence the note of the cuckoo rose musical and soft ; hills, blue in the distance, were seen to the north ; and pretty hamlets, or farm-houses, embosomed in trees, with a little church spire pointing towards heaven, gave the interest of life to the scene.

Ernest looked down from his lofty crag, clothed with shrubs and wild rock-creepers almost to its summit, upon the fair prospect below. The Castle of Fontonore looked so small in the distance that it was almost hidden from view by a hovel that stood on a hill between. The banner on the flag-staff seemed a mere blue speck which the eye could hardly distinguish.

" 'Tis thus," thought its possessor, " that, from the heights of heaven, we may look down upon what we most prize below. How small will our honours appear to us then ! how little all that here we most valued ! " He gazed down on the churchyard, which was not far from the rocks, and thought how glorious a scene would that quiet green spot present, when the seeds there sown in corruption should spring forth into life, and the Lord come to gather in the harvest of His redeemed.

Presently Ernest saw beneath him some one approaching the bridge. His elevation, though considerable, was not so great but that he recognized the face and figure of Jack Lawless. It would take some time to reach him by descending the path. Ernest adopted a shorter way of warning him of danger, and, leaning over the crag, shouted loudly and repeatedly, " Do not try the bridge; it is not safe !" Jack could not help hearing the voice, and looked up;—his only reply was his own audacious smile. Ernest had warned him before of dangers of another kind: he had disregarded the warning then, he disregarded it now. As if he wished to show that he despised any caution given to him by one whom he hated, or, perhaps, led only by the foolish daring of a boy, he set his foot upon the rotten plank, and the next moment was precipitated into the water !

Ernest heard the sharp cry, saw the sudden fall; he knew that the wretched boy could not swim, and that in a few moments he must be hurried over the cataract, and dashed to pieces on the rocks below ! Ernest never paused to consider how slight was the chance of saving him—how great that of losing his own life in the attempt ; still less did he stop to recollect that the miserable Lawless was one who had treated him with insult and hate ; he only saw that a fellow-creature was perishing before him, on the brink of destruction, and *unprepared !* If he descended by the path, his aid must come too late : Ernest took a shorter and more perilous way. Springing from the edge of the crag, swinging himself down by the shrubs that grew on the rock, clinging, leaping, clambering, falling, he descended from the height as never human being had descended before. Twice he dashed himself against the crags in his desperate descent ; a thrill of sharp agony shot across his frame, but now it was impossible to stop. Down he plunged into the water, almost at the head of the fall, at the moment that the current was carrying Lawless over the edge. The left hand of Ernest still grasped the bough of a willow which he had caught as he first struck the stream ; the right, hastily extended, grasped the hair of the drowning boy, and held him back from the fatal brink. But the fearful effort could not last, though it was an effort for life. Ernest felt both his strength and his senses failing him—the exhausted fingers must relax their clasp—both must perish ! No ! no ! there is a loud shout heard—help is near, an eager hand is stretched out to save—a firm hold is laid on the arm of Fontonore —he is dragged to the shore in a senseless state, his livid hand still unconsciously wreathed in the locks of the boy whom he has saved !

"Thank God ! oh, thank God !" exclaimed Mr. Ewart, as he laid the two boys side by side on the turf, dripping, ghastly, insensible, but living still. He hastened for the aid which was speedily afforded. Ernest and Lawless were removed to the nearest cottage, where every means was used to restore them. A messenger was hastily despatched for a doctor, but before he arrived

THE RESCUE.

both of the sufferers had sufficiently recovered to be
taken back to the castle.   Lawless felt no further effect
from his accident than a slight chill and a sense of ex-
haustion ; but it was far otherwise with his youthful
preserver, who had sustained very severe injury in his
dangerous descent, and who awoke to consciousness in a
state of such suffering as excited alarm in the minds of
his friends.

The doctor arrived after some delay, and examined the injured boy, who shrank from his touch in uncontrollable pain. Dr. Mansell looked grave, and drew Mr. Hope aside.

"I should wish, for my own satisfaction," he said, "that other advice should be called in. The case is, I fear, of a serious nature—could not a messenger be despatched upon horseback at once to bring Dr. Ashby?" a surgeon of great eminence, who resided in a town at some distance.

"One shall be sent directly," replied Mr. Hope. "You do not apprehend any danger?" he added, speaking in a low, earnest tone.

"We will say nothing till Dr. Ashby's opinion is given. I hope that there is no cause for alarm;" but the manner of the medical man contradicted his words.

Intense was the anxiety with which Charles and Mr. Ewart awaited the coming of the surgeon. How many, alas, have known that terrible period of waiting for the arrival of the doctor, when minutes seem lengthening into hours—for the life of a loved one is at stake! Charles was in such a state of feverish excitement, that Mr. Hope positively forbade his entering the apartment where the poor sufferer lay. Long before any one else could hear them, he caught the sound of carriage-wheels, and was ready at the bridge to receive the surgeon, whose lips would decide the fate of his brother.

Dr. Ashby was a stout, bald-headed man, with a quick, penetrating eye, and a manner which inspired confidence; decided, without being harsh.   Charles could hardly have been prevented from following him into Ernest's room, in which Mr. Ewart and Dr. Mansell now were, but Mrs. Hope kept him back with the words, "Stay here in the corridor, Charles; the sight of your agitated face would be enough to kill him at once." She entered in, and closed the door gently behind her.

How long, oh, how long appeared the interval! With what different feelings Charles now stood at the door of that room which he had once entered in such grief and resentment on the day of his return from Marshdale!   He then hated the sounds which showed him where his brother was moving through the castle; now his ear was painfully strained to catch any accent of that brother's voice : he was then almost inclined to murmur at the loss of the broad lands which he had once possessed; now, had they been his, he would have given them all to have had Ernest by his side once more.

At length the door opened, and the two doctors came out, followed by Mrs. Hope.   Charles looked the question which his voice could not utter—his aunt laid her finger upon her lips.

"They will consult together in another room," she whispered; "wait here, and I will bring you the result."

With a sickening heart Charles leaned back on the wall opposite the door of Ernest's apartment : he tried to pray, but his mind could scarcely form a prayer—the suspense seemed to paralyze all its energies. After the lapse of some minutes, he heard the rustle of his aunt's dress again : she came close to him, laid her hand on his shoulder, and in a low voice uttered but one sentence: " Charles, you will be Lord of Fontonore ! "

CHAPTER XXVI.

COMING TO THE RIVER.

" Now I further saw, that between them and the gate was a river."
Pilgrim's Progress

"ELL, as you please, but I would not do so," said Mr. Hope, in conversation with Mr. Ewart in the saloon.

"The doctors gave no hope, and I think that in such cases it is only right—it is only kind to let the patient know his danger."

"Your ideas are different to mine: the shock of being told that you are dying is enough to put out the last spark of life."

"Not to one who has the faith of Ernest."

"You would then only hide the truth from a bad man?"

"I would hide it from none; I would act towards others as I should wish them to act towards me. It is cruel to conceal their state from the dying; to send them into the presence of their Maker unwarned, perhaps unprepared."

"Well, you must break the truth to Ernest yourself, I will not undertake to do it. You know his feelings better than I do, I never could understand them at all."

Bowed down with affliction, yet with sufficient self-command to be calm and composed in his manner, Mr. Ewart approached the bedside of Ernest.

"What do the doctors say of me?" asked Fontonore.

"They say that the injuries which you have received are very severe."

"I thought so—I suffer so much pain. I daresay that it will be long before I quite recover. But you see," he added, with a faint smile, "good comes out of evil in this case. I took advantage of the privilege of illness, and the claim which your having saved me has given you, and asked my uncle a favour which he could not refuse me; nor will you, I am sure, dear Mr. Ewart : you will be tutor at Fontonore again ! "

The clergyman pressed in silence the feverish hand held out to him; he could not at that moment reply.

" We shall be so happy, if I only get well ! You do not know how we have missed you ! You will—will you not ?—be the pilgrim's guide again ! "

" You have come to a part of your journey, my beloved pupil, in which God can alone be your guide." He felt that the deep eyes of Ernest were riveted upon him ; he could not endure to meet their inquiring gaze. Shading his own with his hand, he continued : " When

Christian had passed through the land of Beulah, and drew near to the celestial city, he saw a river flowing before him—"

"The river of death!" murmured Ernest, and for some moments there was profound silence in the room. It was first broken by the voice of the sufferer.

"Is there no chance of my recovery?"

"I fear none," faltered the clergyman.

"And how long do the doctors think that this will last?"

"Not many days," replied Mr. Ewart, in a tone scarcely audible.

Again there was a long solemn silence.

"I thank you for telling me this," said Ernest at last. "I little thought that I was so near the end of my pilgrimage—that I was so very near my rest. I have often wondered," he added faintly, "how I should meet this hour—whether in joy, or in trouble and fear. I feel little of either just now—perhaps because I am weak and in pain—but a quiet trust in my Saviour, because, however sinful I have been, I know, I feel that I love Him!"

There are many lying on a sick-bed, who could hardly give a reason for the hope that is in them—whose feeble minds have scarcely power to grasp the simplest text—to whom it would be impossible to review their past lives; but who can yet rest calmly and securely on the thought, " *Lord, Thou knowest all things; Thou knowest that I love Thee !* "

After a while, the sufferer spoke again.

" Where is Charley ?   Why is he not with me ? "

" It was feared that his grief might agitate you."

" Poor dear Charley ! " said Ernest with tenderness ; " it will be a pleasure to him now to think that we always have loved one another.   But I should greatly like to see him ; I have so much to say to him before we part."

" I will call him," said Mr. Ewart, rising.

He found poor Charles weeping at the door.

" You must command yourself, dear boy, for his sake. Ernest has asked to see you."

Charles dashed the drops from his eyes, and made a strong effort to be calm, though the convulsive quivering of his lip showed the intensity of his feelings.   With noiseless step he glided to the bed-side : his brother received him with a faint smile.

" Heaven orders all things well, Charley," he whispered ; " I always felt that you were better fitted than I to be the Lord of Fontonore.   The time which we have spent together will seem to you soon like a strange dream that is past ; but you will not forget me, Charley, mine own brother—you will not forget me ? "

Charles hid his face in his hands.

" And you will be kind to some for my sake.   Poor

Madge! you will not desert her, nor turn away Ben and Jack?"

"I shall never endure the sight of that boy!" exclaimed Charles, in an agitated voice. "He has given you nothing but torment, and now has cost a life ten million times more precious than his own."

"He may have been saved for better things, and then my life will have been well bestowed."

Mr. Ewart left the two brothers alone together, and with a slow, sad step, proceeded along the corridor, proposing to visit the gardener's cottage, to which Jack had now returned.

He met Clementina on the staircase.

"Oh, Mr. Ewart, is it possible—is he really dying?" exclaimed the young lady in unaffected sorrow: "so young, and with everything to make life sweet; it is really too dreadful to think of! Does he know the doctor's opinion?"

"He knows all, and is perfectly tranquil."

"What wonderful strength of mind!"

"The LORD is his strength," replied the clergyman, and passed on.

Many an anxious inquiry after the young lord had Mr. Ewart to answer from different members of the household, before he reached the gardener's cottage. He was desirous to know what effect his own deliverance and Ernest's danger would have upon the mind of young Lawless.

He did not see Jack as he entered the cottage, and asked the gardener's wife where he was.

"Oh, he's there on the bed, sir, with his face to the wall. He's never moved, nor spoken, nor tasted a morsel, since he heard that the young lord lay a-dying. I can't get him to answer a question ; he lies there as still as a stone. I can't say if he feels it or not, he has such a strange sullen way."

Mr. Ewart seated himself close to the boy, who appeared to take no notice of his presence.

"You are not suffering, I hope, from your fall ? Yours has been a wonderful preservation ; but for the generous courage of Lord Fontonore, you would have been now before the judgment-seat of God."

Lawless gave no sign that he heard him.

"I have just quitted his sick-room," continued the clergyman. "He is quite calm in the prospect of death, for his life has for long been one preparation for it. The last words that I heard him utter were of you ;—he was recommending you to the kindness of his brother."

Lawless convulsively clutched his pillow.

"He said," added Mr. Ewart, "that if you were but saved for better things, his life would have been well bestowed."

Jack suddenly half raised himself upon his bed, then dashed himself down again with frantic violence. "I can't bear this," he cried, in a choking voice. "I wish he would hate me, abuse me, trample upon me ; anything would be better than this !"

Yes, under all the deep crust of selfishness, malice, and pride, lay a spring of feeling, in the depths of that unconverted heart. That spring had been reached, the deep buried waters gushed forth, and the clergyman left the cottage with a faint but precious hope that his loved pupil had not suffered in vain.

CHAPTER XXVII.

" The foundation upon which the city was framed was higher than the clouds; they therefore went up through the regions of the air, sweetly talking as they went, being comforted because they safely got over the river, and had such glorious companions to attend them."—*Pilgrim's Progress.*

T would be unnecessary, as well as painful, to mark every step of the progress of the young Pilgrim through the last stage of his earthly journey. He had no mental doubts or gloom ; his mind was calm and unclouded, sometimes so vividly realizing the joy set before him that bodily pain seemed almost forgotten. Often he appeared buried in thought, as though his spirit were already holding converse with things unseen, before quitting the frail suffering body.

" Charles," said he one night to his brother, who sat bathing his temples with vinegar and water, " how gently and lovingly the picture of my mother seems to look on me now. Perhaps she is waiting to welcome me on the blissful shore, where there is no more parting and pain. You will lay me in the vault beside her."

Charles breathed a heavy sigh.

"I have been thinking of that monument," continued Ernest, "so strangely prepared for the living. But the lines upon it could never suit me now—'the mists of earth' have long since stained 'the snow-flake.'"

"It is more spotless than ever," whispered Charles: "is it not written, *Though your sins be as scarlet, they shall be as white as snow ; though they be red like crimson, they shall be as wool ?*"

"Yes," murmured the sufferer ; "Jesus can present sinners faultless before the presence of his Father. He has *loved us, and washed us in His own precious blood.* This is all my hope." After a short silence, he continued —"My eyes are heavy with long waking, dear Charley. I wish that I could hear you sing to me once more ; I feel as though it would soothe this dull pain."

"I do not think that I could sing now."

"Not one little hymn—my favourite hymn ? But if the effort pains you, do not try."

But Charles did try, though with unsteady voice, whose tones sounded strange to himself. In the quiet night, with no listener near but one sufferer on earth, and the happy angels above, he sang this simple evening hymn :—

H Y M N.

After labour, how sweet is rest!
Gently the weary eyelids close :

As the infant sleeps on its mother's breast,
    The child of God may in peace repose.
Whether we sleep, or whether we wake,
We are His who gave His life for our sake.

He to whom darkness is as light,
    Tenderly guards His slumbering sheep ;
The Shepherd watches His flock by night,
    The feeble lambs He will safely keep.
Whether we sleep, or whether we wake,
We are His who gave His life for our sake.

Death's night comes ; it may now be near :
    Lord, if our hopes are fixed on Thee,
Oh, how calm will that sleep appear!
    Oh, how sweet will the waking be !
Whether we sleep, or whether we wake,
We are His who gave His life for our sake.

The eyes of Ernest gradually closed ere the hymn was ended ; he lay still in deep slumbers ; Charles almost trembled lest that slumber should be death.

" I have bidden farewell to Ben ; I must see his brother also.   Dying words have sometimes weight—he may listen to me now.   Please raise me higher on my pillow, and call in Jack to see me."

Such were the words of Ernest, on awaking one morning more free from pain than he had been since his fall.

" The interview will not be too much for you, Ernest ? " said Mr. Ewart, anxiously.

"Oh, no; nothing can hurt me now. I feel as though nothing could agitate me again. Have you seen my cousin lately?" he added.

"Yes; only this morning. She feels this trial much."

"Does she?" exclaimed Ernest, a look of animation and pleasure lighting up his deep sunken eye. "Oh, tell Clementina that she must come to me too. My heart is so full of thoughts—if I only could utter them ! Would that I had the tongue of an angel, but for this one day —before I am silenced by death !"

"Lawless is at the door, as you wished," said Charles.

"Pray, then, leave us alone together for a few minutes, and then return with Clementina, dear brother, if she is not afraid to come near a death-bed ; it will be a new and a strange scene to her."

Jack stood at the door, as if fearful to come in, like the sinner who dreads that he is beyond reach of hope. He could hardly believe himself to be an object of deep interest to one whom he had so cruelly wronged and in-sulted, for there was nothing in his own corrupted heart to lead him to understand free mercy and goodness.

There was something painfully oppressive to the boy in the aspect of that darkened room, coming out, as he did, from the bright sunshine. The noiseless manner in which Mr. Ewart and Charles quitted the apartment; the solemn stillness that pervaded the place; the look of the little table beside the bed, covered with things that reminded of illness and pain; the appearance of the sufferer himself, almost as colourless as the pillow upon which he lay; the lines of death written on his calm, pale features, so that even a child could not mistake them—all struck a chill to the heart of Lawless. He almost felt as though he were Ernest's murderer.

"Come nearer," said Fontonore, faintly ; "my time is short; I wish to speak to you a few words before I die."

"You must not—shall not, die for me!" exclaimed the boy, in stifled tones of anguish, as he knelt beside the bed.

"Think not of me now ;—-I would tell you—if God grant me strength—I would tell you of One who has died indeed for sinners—for you—for me. For those who have insulted Him, and despised His warnings—for those who have hardened their hearts against His mercy ; even for such the Son of God stooped to die. Oh, can you resist a love such as this?" The once proud, insolent boy was sobbing aloud.

"See, here is my Bible, my precious Bible; I am going where even that will be needed no more. I give it to you—keep it as a remembrance of me. Will you promise me to read it, for my sake ? "

"For your sake," groaned Lawless, " I would do anything ! I can never, never forget what you have done and suffered for me."

JACK RECEIVING THE BIBLE.

"Oh, rather remember what the High and Holy One has done and suffered for us both. Your heart is touched with feeling for me; you are grateful towards a poor worm of earth, and can you remain hardened and rebellious towards the merciful Saviour, who is now stretching out His arms to call you to Himself. Who is so ready to receive you, so ready to forgive, as He who has sacrificed His life, that you may live!"

The boy could make no reply; but the dying words then heard were branded on his soul, never to be forgotten while memory should endure.

"Come in, dear Clemmy; it is very kind in you to visit the sick-room," murmured Ernest. Followed by Charles and Mr. Ewart, Clementina entered, mingled pity, fear, and awe on her face. Fontonore held out to his cousin his white, emaciated hand.

"You will be better soon, I trust," faltered the young lady.

"Yes; I shall *be with Christ, which is far better.*"

"But it is terrible to leave all—so early—it seems so cruel! Ernest, you are too young for—for death!"

"Too young for happiness, my cousin? Do you remember our conversation in London; how I told you that none could be happy as the Christian, that there is no pleasure equal to what religion can give? I thought it then," he cried, his voice strengthening, his eye kindling as he spoke; "I thought it then, Clementina, but I *know* it now! What is it to me that I bear the title of a peer, that this castle is mine, that men call me great —I must leave all, perhaps before the sun sets; I must leave all, and yet my whole soul is full of joy—joy beyond all that earth can ever bestow. I am passing through the river, but it does not overflow me; beneath are the everlasting arms—before me are the glories of the eternal city, where I shall see Him whom not seeing I have loved!"

There was a radiance upon the dying countenance that seemed not of earth but heaven. Clementina looked upon Ernest, wondering; and for the first time felt the littleness of the world, and the vanity of all that it can give.

"Where is my Pilgrim's Progress?" continued Fontonore, more faintly. "Cousin, I have reserved it for you. When this frail body is laid in the grave, then read it, and think of one weak Pilgrim who trod the path to the Celestial City with feeble steps, too often, alas! turning aside from the way; yet on whom the Lord of Pilgrims had great mercy, whom the Saviour guided by His counsel here—and afterward—received—into glory!"

Ernest sank back on his pillow exhausted. A change came over his features; there was breathless silence in the room.

"He is going!" murmured Mr. Ewart, clasping his hands.

Ernest unclosed his eyes, fixed a long last look of inexpressible love on his brother; then, turning it towards the clergyman, faintly uttered the single word "Pray!"

At once all sank on their knees, every distinction forgotten in that solemn hour. The heir of a peerage—

the vain child of fashion, bent side by side with the convict's son! Mr. Ewart's voice was raised in prayer : he commended the parting spirit to his Saviour, while Fontonore's upward gaze, and the motion of his silent lips, showed that he heard and joined in the prayer. Presently that motion ceased—the light faded from that eye, the silver cord was gently unloosed ; but the smile which still lingered on the features of the dead seemed an earnest of the bliss of the freed, rejoicing spirit, safely landed on the shores of Eternity.

CHAPTER XXVIII.

IT may not, perhaps, be uninteresting to the reader to trace a little of the future career of those whom Ernest left behind him in the world.

Charles, of course, inherited the title and estate of his brother, and, increasing in piety and virtue as he increased in years, became an ornament to the high station in which he was placed, and a blessing to the people amongst whom he dwelt. He carried out all Ernest's projects of charity with zeal; and when, on attaining the age of twenty-one, the management of his own estate came into his hands, he erected the church upon his grounds which he had designed so long before, and often listened within its walls to the words of truth from the lips of his early preceptor.

For Madge and Ben Charles procured respectable situations, and would have done the same for their brother; but the wish of the boy was to be a soldier, and accordingly, when old enough, he enlisted. Blunt and rough as he remained, the conduct of the youth showed the power of Christianity even in a hard, rugged nature. The life of Ernest had not been thrown away, nor had his prayers been unheard.

After many years of service in his own country, Lawless embarked with his regiment for the Crimea, and was present at the engagement of the Alma. As he rushed on, one of the foremost in the action, he received a musket-ball on his chest, and fell, as his comrades believed, never to rise more. How was it that he sprang again from the ground, uninjured and undismayed? The Russian ball had struck him, indeed, but had found a bloodless resting-place—it had lodged in the Bible which he carried in his breast, the dying gift of Ernest of Fontonore!

Mr. Hope sank under an attack of apoplexy, a few years after the death of his nephew. The man of the world was called away in the midst of his business, his schemes of ambition, at the time that he had attained the object of his hopes, by being elected member for Allborough. The expenses of his canvass, and residence in town, and the extravagance in which his wife had indulged, had ruined a fortune which had never been a large one ; and Mrs. Hope had the misery, intolerable to her proud spirit, of passing the rest of her days a dependant on the generosity of her nephew. Truly might she say, in reviewing her past life, " *Vanity of vanities, all is vanity !* "

And what was the fate of the pretty, affected Clementina, the butterfly hovering over the blossoms of pleasure?

Let us pass over the space of nearly twenty years, and behold the vain young beauty as she appears now that the first silver lines begin to streak her auburn hair, and all the gay visions of her youth have faded for ever.

Let us enter unseen that low parsonage house, from which comes the merry sound of youthful voices. The snow on the ground, the chill in the air, the red firelight flickering so cheerfully through the diamond-paned window overhung with ivy, all tell that the season is winter. The room in which we find ourselves seems all too small for the party of happy, noisy children assembled within it. This is the first day of the new year, and a merry day it is to the family in Oakdale parsonage. Unfailing is the arrival of the welcome box, which at this season finds its way from Fontonore, and every one is present to witness its opening, from the ruddy schoolboy, home for the holidays, to the little infant in arms. Even the pale-faced pastor himself has laid aside his book and closed his desk, to join in the innocent mirth of his children: you might know him, by the likeness which he bears to her, to be the brother of Ellen Searle.

But who is the thin, careworn-looking mother, who appears in the centre of the merry group? Is it possible to recognize in that quiet parson's wife, in her simple cap, and her plain woollen dress, the once gay Clementina ? What a wondrous change has been wrought by change of circumstances—or rather, by religious principles and domestic affection! Clementina's home is now her world, and the wants of her large family, and the claims of the poor, leave little margin for show. Yet there is a cheerfulness in her tone, and a sweetness in her smile, which in earlier days neither had possessed ; the merry voices of her children, her husband's kind words, and the blessings of the humble members of his flock, far more than make up to her for the now half-forgotten flatteries and follies of Vanity Fair.

To the eldest boy the post of honour is committed. He draws out parcel after parcel from the depths of the box, and calling out aloud the name labelled upon each, gives it to its eager proprietor.

"Mamma, this is for you," and a square, flat parcel, was placed in the hands of Clementina Searle. It contained two small framed paintings by Charles, to adorn the bare walls of her humble little home. Perhaps there was something in the subject of those drawings which recalled thoughts of former days, for the lady's eyes grew moist as she looked upon them.

The one represented a mossy ruin, gray with age, and near it a rustic gate, on which leaned a youthful pilgrim. A staff was in his hand, a burden on his back,

THE WELCOME BOX.

and he was looking upwards, with an anxious eye, on the cloudy, lowering sky above him.

The other represented a clear broad river, glittering in the rays of the setting sun. Beyond it were banks clothed with verdure and beauty, with a rich, red glow over all, and the openings between the wreaths of golden clouds seemed to give glimpses of brighter glories beyond. The same pilgrim appeared, one foot still in the stream, the other on the beautiful shore ; his face could not be seen, but the sunny beams shone like a halo round his head ; the burden was gone, and instead of the staff his hand grasped the conqueror's palm.

"How fondly he is remembered yet," thought

Clementina; "the brother's love seems but to strengthen with time." She was interrupted by the voice of her son Ernest.

"Mamma, see what a beautiful book Mr. Ewart has sent me ! It looks like an old friend in a new dress,

THE NEW BOOK.

for I am sure that it is just the same as the one that you read to us on Sundays, only that mine is so prettily bound and illustrated, so I like it much better than your's."

"No binding could add to the value of mine," replied the mother, with a gentle sigh ; "it was given to me by a dear friend now in heaven, who was the first to teach me from its pages the way to the Celestial City. In the life and death of that young servant of God, early called to his endless rest, but not until his work was done, I find pictures of the scenes described in that book—they are to me ILLUSTRATIONS OF THE PILGRIM'S PROGRESS!"

And now, dear Reader, you who have traced with me the steps of the Young Pilgrim, through the various stages of his mortal life, suffer one word from your friend ere we part. Do you know anything of the pilgrimage of which you have here read? I ask not, Have you walked soberly through Vanity Fair, keeping yourself *unspotted from the world?*—if you have struggled with Apollyon, and been conqueror in the fight, or passed with a firm and unflinching step through the Valley of the Shadow of Death? But have you stood beneath the cross of the Saviour, and found its power to remove the burden of sin? Have you ever even felt that sin *is* a burden, and knocked earnestly at the gate of Mercy? Or are you yet dwelling in the City of Destruction, thinking, caring nothing for the things belonging to your peace, laughing at the idea of a pilgrimage to Heaven, or putting it off for a more convenient season? Oh, for the sake of your own immortal soul, awake to your danger ere it be too late! The wicket-gate of Mercy is still opened to prayer; the blood which flowed from the cross still can wash away sin; the Holy Spirit is still willing to guide your steps on the narrow way, up the Hill of Difficulty, down the Valley of Humiliation, through sunshine and darkness, through life and through death—to the eternal mansions prepared for you in Heaven !

www.ingramcontent.com/pod-product-compliance
Lightning Source LLC
Chambersburg PA
CBHW030626030726
47497CB00006B/1648